Surviving the Evacuation
Book 1: London

Frank Tayell

Dedicated to my family

Published by Frank Tayell
Copyright 2013
All rights reserved

All people, places, and (especially) events are fictional.

ISBN-13: 978-1492861119
ISBN-10: 1492861111

Other titles:

Post-Apocalyptic Detective Novels
Strike a Match 1. Serious Crimes
Strike a Match 2. Counterfeit Conspiracy
Strike a Match3: Endangered Nation
Work. Rest. Repeat.

Surviving The Evacuation/Here We Stand
Book 1: London
Book 2: Wasteland
Zombies vs The Living Dead
Book 3: Family
Book 4: Unsafe Haven
Book 5: Reunion
Book 6: Harvest
Book 7: Home
Here We Stand 1: Infected & 2: Divided
Book 8: Anglesey
Book 9: Ireland
Book 10: The Last Candidate
Book 11: Search and Rescue
Book 12: Britain's End

For more information, visit:
http://blog.franktayell.com
www.facebook.com/TheEvacuation

Part 1:
How The End Began

13th March - 16th April

07:09, 13th March, Sydenham, London

Zombies. It seems as strange to read the word as it does to write it. Perhaps when I look back on this diary from the safety of an island or coastal enclave, we'll have come up with a more scientific term. Until then, they— No, make that They. They are zombies. People are attacked, bitten, and infected. They die, then They come back with only one goal, to attack and infect others.

My name is Bartholomew Wright, though most people call me Bill. This journal was the doctor's idea. She said writing down my thoughts and feelings would help me vent without snapping at my loved ones. She was talking about my broken leg, not the undead that have taken over most of the world.

It's twenty-one days since that first outbreak in New York, eighteen since I returned from the hospital. It's seven days since the inland cities of Britain were evacuated, and less than one day since the power went out. I didn't notice at first, not until I realised the kettle hadn't boiled. I checked the television, the fridge, the lamp, and flicked the light switches on and off for at least half an hour. I tried each socket, plugging in every device and charger I could find. When nothing worked, I stared at the streetlights, hoping they would come on. They didn't.

The evacuation was meant to start on the 7th March, but as soon as the twenty-four-hour warning was given on the 6th, everyone began to leave. I watched people walk by all afternoon and long into the night. Some were alone, and some were in small groups. Some travelled light, carrying a small bag, or no bags at all. Others pushed prams and bicycles laden with more than they could carry. By dawn, the streets were once again deserted.

They'd said that the power would be diverted from the cities as soon as the evacuation was complete. As the days went by and my heater still worked, my kettle boiled, and the nights were bathed in the streetlights' sickly orange glow, I foolishly came to believe that they'd left the power on just for me. They hadn't. The lights in London went out yesterday afternoon. They won't be coming back on.

3

I work, or worked, as a political advisor, mostly and most recently for Jennifer Masterton, MP. Jen and I have known each other since we were children. After university we set up a consultancy firm together. We were full of the usual ideas of changing the world, of ending hunger, curing disease, and eradicating poverty. We planned to achieve all this through a policy shop whose only credibility came from having her father, a former chancellor, listed on the letterhead.

Our firm barely lasted six months, just long enough for her to include it on her CV when she stood in the Bygrave North by-election. She won by a landslide. I couldn't believe it, nor could she. Her father couldn't believe that she'd broken with generations of family tradition and won the seat for 'The Dishonourable Enemy', as he called them.

Her election meant the end of our partnership. I carried on alone, and she felt guilty enough to throw work my way. I didn't get rich, not even close, but I managed to keep the bank manager happy. As her star rose, I began to gain a small reputation of my own. Perhaps out of that same guilt, she didn't often correct journalists when I introduced myself as the mastermind behind her success.

Jen was the reason I was walking down a Whitehall staircase at 16:30 GMT on the 20th February at the same time as an RAF uniform was barrelling up it. I was knocked over the banister to the cold marble floor twenty feet below. I know the time, and know I'll remember it, because that's when the reports from New York started coming in.

I was unconscious for three nights. When I woke, I found myself in an empty hospital ward with an armed soldier at the foot of the bed, another by the door, and Jen sitting by the bedside. They were her protection detail. All ministers now had them, and Jen had been appointed Minister for the Interior in the eight-member coalition cabinet.

Her eyes were red. She looked oddly distracted as she glanced through a folder stamped 'Top Secret'. When she saw I was awake, Jen called for a doctor. I received a cursory examination that went into barely more depth than ensuring I knew who I was, where I was, and that I understood that my right leg was broken. Jen dismissed the doctor, and then checked that no one but her bodyguard was in earshot. Then she said that something terrible had happened. She took a laptop from her bag, queued up a video, told me to watch, and then returned her attention to her folder.

It took a moment for me to realise I was watching a clip from a newsfeed. Across the bottom of the screen ran a ticker that read 'Biological Attack in New York State', 'At Least Ten Attacks', 'Weapon of Unknown Origin'. The footage taking up most of the screen had been shot from a helicopter, and showed an outdoor seating area on the second floor of a mall. A crowd was streaming from the building, but there was no indication why. There was no smoke, no fire, just hundreds of people pushing and shoving their way onto a balcony designed to seat a few dozen. Meanwhile, through the tinny speakers, a news-anchor repeated the few scant details: an unknown threat; attacks throughout the northeastern U.S.; the president was going to issue a statement shortly; airports were closed, and on and on. This litany from the studio only ceased when people began jumping off the roof.

The camera had pulled back so the screen showed the entire front of the mall and the mass of people flooding into the car park. When the first bodies fell, they were just indistinct shapes. It took a few seconds for the camera operator to react and zoom in on the balcony. A group of teens in high-school sports jackets overturned tables in a futile attempt to barricade the doors. They hadn't noticed that, just ten yards away, zombies were staggering through a restaurant and out onto the balcony. As the improvised barricade got higher, the undead got closer. Looking for something else to add to the barrier, one of the teenagers turned around and came face to face with one of the undead.

It wasn't like a horror film, not like any I've ever seen. The zombie didn't just grab and paw at clothing, it clawed at the young man, ignoring his desperate blows as it gripped his flesh, dragged itself closer, and bit down on his shoulder. An arc of blood sprayed up, and the image blurred, moving away from the struggle. Perhaps there had been some instruction from the studio, or perhaps the operator had had enough of that particularly gruesome scene.

The picture tightened on a man and a woman near the edge of the roof. They probably weren't an actual couple. In all that chaotic confusion, it's probable that they'd never met before, and he just acted out of some ingrained archaic chivalry. He pushed the woman behind him, putting himself between her and the snarling monster, its face masked red with the blood of its previous victims.

He was a large man, well over six feet tall, and looked like he'd been an athlete before a few sedentary decades had turned muscle to fat, but he was still twice the size of the zombie creeping ever closer. I watched as he braced himself, as he straightened his back, squared his shoulders, tightened his jaw, clenched his fist, and threw a right hook straight into the zombie's face. He'd put his entire weight into the punch and it was a good one, a solid blow that knocked the creature off its feet. As he clenched and unclenched his hand against the pain of the blow, there was a look of triumph in his eyes and a satisfied smile on his face. It disappeared when a snarling blonde in a security uniform lurched into the gap.

The man picked up a chair and swung it at head height, knocking the security guard down, but then there was another, and another, and a dozen more zombies behind those. Tears rolled down the man's face as he swung again and again, knocking Them down, but They didn't notice. They didn't even flinch. As one fell and struggled to get up, there were always more waiting to take its place.

He was totally focused on the threat in front, and couldn't have realised what he was doing. With each swing he took a half-step back. I don't think the woman he was protecting knew how close she was to the edge, not until he swung, pushed her back another pace, and this time her foot found nothing but air. She grabbed at him. Her mouth opened in a scream. As his head turned, as he saw the woman fall, as he reached out to catch her, the undead security guard lurched forward and tore at his throat.

The picture wobbled before flicking down to the woman, now lying in the parking lot. If the fall *had* killed her, it would have been a more merciful death than that of her erstwhile saviour, but she was still alive. Her legs were twisted at an odd angle. Her head swivelled from side to side as she tried to see behind her, back towards the main doors where the flood of fleeing people was turning to the slower lumbering stream of the living dead.

The camera zoomed out to show more of the parking lot. Bodies kept falling onto the asphalt as people jumped or were pushed. Fights broke out as cars were stolen. Other vehicles were abandoned as the road became jammed. The drivers and passengers, now become pedestrians, punched and pushed their way ahead of others, not knowing whether safety lay ahead, but certain that death followed behind. The injured woman was now just a distant shape. I couldn't make out her face. It didn't matter. I won't forget it. She was somebody's daughter, perhaps somebody's mother.

Then it happened, the moment when I truly began to understand what it was I was seeing, how an impossible nightmare had become stark reality. One of the fallen bodies got to its knees and began to drag itself towards her. It couldn't have been alive, not with a jagged shard of metal protruding from its chest. It was impossible. It was terrible. It was unbelievable, but it was happening. Someone who should be dead, wasn't. It clawed its way towards the unfortunate woman, its intention clear.

She must have heard it approaching. Her head twisted violently back and forth. Her hands scrabbled frantically against the concrete as she tried to drag herself away. Her head bucked as the creature grabbed at her ankle. She screamed as it pulled itself up her legs and tore at her flesh with its half-ruined mouth.

Finally the camera pulled way back, showing the shopping mall, the access roads, and the industrial estate next door. Individual figures were too small to discern, it was just a great mass of humanity flowing out, some in cars, some on foot. Following was an inexorable wave, growing in size as some of those who had died rose up and joined the pursuit.

When the video stopped, I looked over at Jen. "It's everywhere," she said. "There's no cure." Then she bent forward and whispered, "And it's here, too."

It's twenty-one days since the outbreak in New York. Eighteen days since I left the hospital, seven since I watched the evacuees walking through the street below, and three since my last contact with the outside world. That was a text from Jen to say a car was being sent to pick me up. The car came. It's still there. The driver is dead.

09:00, 13th March

I can only see a couple of Them down in the street. No, three. There are three zombies out in the open, but I think there are more hidden in the front gardens of the houses on the opposite side of the road. I can see the bushes moving slightly, but that could be the wind, right?

It took me the best part of an hour to get over to the window. I don't know if it was worth the effort. Yes, yes, of course it's worth it. Lack of information breeds fear and I don't need any more of that. I had to pull myself over on the wheeled desk-chair. That's my only way to get around except for the crutches, but there's not enough space up here for those to be anything other than a hindrance.

A proper cast would have been nice. This thing's like something out of the 1940s. They didn't even pin my leg, which means when the cast does come off, I'll be lucky if I ever walk properly again. Typical NHS! That was an attempt at humour. It doesn't work, does it? I just feel so trapped here, so on edge. I've always hated waiting. Every time I hear a sound in the distance, I'm sure it's the car coming to rescue me.

It didn't really take me an hour to get across to the window. At most it was ten minutes, but everything takes so much longer than it used to, and seems to take even longer than that. Whenever I do find a position in which I can be vaguely comfortable, I forget the leg's in plaster, try to move it normally, and smack it against the wall or the side of the desk.

I'm glad I've got the painkillers. Forty-three nasty little blue pills. Forty-two now. Should I start rationing them? It might be a while before I get any more.

The government car, the one Jen sent, is still there, by my front gate. If I'd been able to speak to her, I'd have warned her about the undead outside. I would have told her it wasn't safe. I did try calling. I've tried since, but there's no answer.

The mobile phone networks were shut down just after the footage started coming out of New York. The news initially reported that the networks were overloaded, then they claimed that the frequencies were being temporarily re-allocated to the emergency services. Jen left me a government-issue phone, one she said would work regardless of any emergency. When I couldn't get through to her, I tried ringing every number I could remember, every number in my phone book, and every number I could find. I have a few old magazines, and called the numbers they gave for subscriptions. No one answered. I've turned the phone off. Who knows how long the battery will last? Jen knows where I am, and she knows I'm waiting.

09:40, 13th March

What do I know about the undead? Not much. The outbreak began in New York and quickly spread. They can be killed. Technically They are already dead. Certainly, They are no longer human. They feel no pain, and as far as anyone has been able to tell, They can't communicate. They are not immortal, but They can withstand far greater trauma than any living person, and They only stop when their brains are destroyed. Someone who's been infected can live anywhere from a few minutes up to a few hours before dying. After death, They come back. How long it takes for someone to succumb to the infection doesn't seem to be linked to the severity of their wounds. I've seen footage of people missing limbs who've languished in pain for hours and those who've received the merest scratch turning almost instantly.

Like I said, I don't know much. Jen sent me copies of the dossiers the intelligence services put together, but they contained scant few facts and a lot of speculation. Most of my information came from a fixer whom I only knew as Sholto, via an online drop-box.

Sholto and I first crossed paths about seven years ago. I never learned his real name. After the fourth message, when he was shaking me down over what was really nothing more than a misunderstanding, I asked what I should call him. He said Sholto. About a month later, I finally got around to picking up the Sherlock Holmes anthology that Jen had given me for Christmas. It had sat on the coffee table since the holidays, unwrapped but unread. Inside was a bookmark, an Orwellian 'Big Brother Is Watching You!'. After seeing the page it marked, I tore the flat apart looking for bugs. I never found any, but that's not to say they weren't there.

The exact details of what I did or didn't do, whether or not it was in anyway unethical, because it wasn't illegal, not really… well, the specifics aren't important, not now. Let's just say I owed him. He'd get in touch every once in a while, sometimes offering something, sometimes asking for something. Since what he usually asked for was worth a lot less to me than what he offered, I kept in touch. It was thanks to his information that Jen climbed the greasy pole, but though I told Jen that I had a source, I never told her everything I learned from him. I suspect he worked for the CIA, the NSA, MI6, GCHQ, or some other acronym, though I never found out which. He was male, he was from the U.S., and he liked playing chess online at ungodly hours. That's all I really know about him. We were never friends. The only time he called on the phone he used a voice synthesiser, and I'm old fashioned enough to think that true friends know what each other sound like. But there were times, usually late at night, when I'd get these odd messages which made me think that this guy, whoever and wherever he was, genuinely didn't have anyone else.

During the journey home from the hospital, Jen summarised what had happened while I'd been unconscious, but the presence of her two uniformed guards limited how much she was free to divulge. She left me with a box of food, the phone, and a promise to return as soon as she could. I tried to sleep, but whenever I closed my eyes, images of that massacre at the mall flooded my brain. After a couple of hours of staring at the ceiling, my painkiller-addled mind slowly processing what Jen had said, I struggled out of bed, and turned on my laptop.

There were twenty messages from Sholto. None were particularly friendly, though few of his missives ever were. The first read, 'I see you're in hospital. When you get out, download these files. Keep them safe. It could be important.'

I'm not sure why I followed his instructions, but I did. Day after day, I copied the files to my laptop, deleting all the documents, films, and music to make room. When the broadband stopped working, I used the government phone. By the time that stopped working, just after the evacuation began, I'd filled the laptop and the external hard drive on which I'd been storing our plans for the election campaign.

I did look at some of the files before the power went out. I listened to the air-traffic control audio-feed from when Air Force Two went down. There were calls between the fire crews when the South Korean oil refineries in Yeosu and Ulsan blew up. I looked at the satellite pictures of the explosion when an oil tanker crashed into the docks in Baltimore. Some of it was in English, some was in Chinese, some in Russian, others in languages I couldn't begin to even guess at. It's all there, out of the way under the bed, and it's interesting, at least the parts I can understand.

Sholto's real genius lay in tracking the outbreak's spread. After I fed his data to Jen, I found that he had a more accurate handle on it than any of our analysts. You've heard the expression 'the shot that was heard around the world?' That came at 18:15 GMT on the second day. The shot was fired by a gendarme straight into the head of an infected tour guide on the Champs-Elysees. Paris was in flames by nightfall.

By the time I woke up in hospital, Britain was under quarantine. No unauthorised flights were being allowed to land, no ferries or ships that hadn't already been secured at sea were allowed to dock, and the Channel Tunnel had been blown up.

Any planes without clearance, and there were lots of those, were shot down while they were still over water. The public were told that most flights were diverted, and the shooting down of aircraft was a last resort. However, no secret was being made of the destruction of air traffic, quite the opposite. By the evening of the 22nd, on all the news stations and news sites that were still operating, footage was broadcast of a jumbo-jet being destroyed above the English Channel. Over the video, the Beeb anchor said, "A Boeing 747 out of Nairobi was targeted by the RAF after an outbreak spread to the flight-deck. The pilot's last transmission was to request the plane be destroyed, as he had been infected. This is the second such incident today." The ticker at the bottom of the screen read 'Breaking News: Another Threat Averted!'

It was such obvious propaganda, so archaic, so reminiscent of the newsreel footage from the Second World War, that I wonder why people accepted it. I suppose because they wanted to believe that the government was still in control and, after all, who cares about Johnny Foreigner, just as long as Tommy is all right?

The Tube was sealed, trains were cancelled, churches, synagogues, and mosques were ordered not to open their doors. Pubs, restaurants, schools, universities, cinemas, theatres, airports, and ferry terminals; anywhere that gave people a reason to congregate was firmly closed. The Army was deployed to guard the supermarkets and empty the petrol stations. People were asked, very politely at first, to go home and listen for announcements as to when they would reopen. The independent stores, corner shops, and mini-marts were allowed to sell whatever they liked at whatever price they could get, but there wouldn't be any deliveries to restock the shelves.

I was impressed by how quick our response was. No, that's not quite right, surprised is closer to the mark. I was surprised by how quickly the Army was deployed, the Channel Tunnel sealed, and the decision taken to destroy all those aircraft and ships. These decisions, I know, aren't made overnight. Jen said there'd been rumours of a terrorist bio-attack for months, aimed at cutting the UK off from the rest of the world. Plans had been put in place to mitigate its impact. I knew she was lying, and she knew I knew. Perhaps it was the presence of her armed guard, but I couldn't get the truth out of her. I don't suppose it matters now.

The curfew ran from six p.m. to six a.m., and martial law was imposed. Looting, or breach of any of the emergency laws, was punishable by an automatic twenty years of hard labour. Breaking the curfew was punishable by death. The few fledgling riots, protests, and demonstrations that sprang up were brutally stamped down. People were shot on sight. That's a bloodless sentence to describe it, but I wasn't there. I didn't see it. I didn't experience the fear, loss, confusion, and panic of those first few days.

It was repeated over and over that, since the undead were incapable of understanding an instruction to stay inside, anyone outside must be infected. There is a hard logic to that, one that tapped so deeply into the fears of the populace, it became the only justification the authorities needed.

The supermarkets reopened as Food Distribution Centres on the 22nd February, first to sell perishable goods, then other items as they became available. Most people didn't keep much food in their homes. 'Just in time shopping', I guess they called it. The Distribution Centres just couldn't meet the demand. Some food got through, and some people got lucky and got a ration, but most went hungry, while others fled. To counter that, they broadcast segments from a Temporary Processing Centre. It was a grand name for a warehouse with row upon row of camp beds where those without one of the coveted travel permits were sent.

You were only allowed to leave if you had a permit, and the news made it clear that if you tried to leave you would have to show it. The footage was bizarre, a mix of public service announcement and reality TV schadenfreude as cars were pulled over and drivers questioned. These segments were never live. I think they'd been carefully selected to find the most expensive cars and most obnoxious passengers.

The police would make a performance out of asking for the permit. Of course, the driver never had one. The car's occupants were bundled into the back of a lorry while the reporter explained to the viewers that the curfew breakers were being taken to a Temporary Processing Centre. In the back of the shot, while the journalist was talking, the car was unceremoniously shoved into a ditch. It was all very theatrical. I doubt they really pushed cars off the road. I mean, why would they when they could be driven somewhere they'd cause less of an obstruction?

Perhaps those people who left early had the right idea. A few days on a hard cot in a cold warehouse would have been better than the long trek of the evacuation. Those curfew breakers would have been among the first wave to be resettled in an enclave, working harder than they'd ever imagined, but they would have been safe.

"There are currently no reported cases in the United Kingdom, Ireland, or the Channel Islands." They broadcast that quite clearly at the beginning of each news bulletin. Then they would list the number of boats sunk and planes shot down, and which new government in exile we were playing host to along with what fraction of its military. I suppose this gave some legitimacy to our salvage operations, the polite euphemism for the piratical theft of ship-borne cargo and the land-based stores designated as food aid for the year's projected global famines. I think all it did was remind people that the world on the other side of the water had fallen over the brink.

Then again, I don't think many people were getting their news from the TV or radio, not in those first few days. Internet traffic spiked as the nation stayed glued to footage from webcams and shaky smartphones, uploaded often without any comment or description beyond a location, and that was all you needed to plot the outbreak's spread.

Governments everywhere claimed to be in control. The pictures told a different story as communities blocked roads, and towns walled themselves in. Armies deserted battalions at a time. Millions fled, and were killed out of fear they were infected. Military crackdowns, summary executions, and food riots followed. It was the same almost everywhere.

The news from China was odd. Not much got out, and the little that did seemed like it had been written in advance. It was as if someone had decided that was going to be the week they'd announce a Yangtze clean-up was going to begin, and they were going to release that to the world regardless of whether there was any global press left who cared. All the Western social media sites were blocked. On their local sites, they'd blocked anything connected with the words zombies, undead, virus, infection, and every other synonym you could imagine.

People were recording and uploading footage, but it never got published. I don't read Mandarin. I don't speak it either, but the footage Sholto pulled from there was as bad as anywhere else. Adults and children, peasants and farmers, professionals and the elite, relative, friend, neighbour, or stranger, infected or not, there's footage of people killing each other as the country was consumed by panic.

The outbreak didn't start in China, despite what the conspiracy theorists would like you to think. They just fed off the silence, wanting to look anywhere but their own back garden, or back *yard*. It started in New York. The outbreak in that mall was part of the second wave, started by someone directly infected by Patient Zero.

Who exactly Patient Zero was, I don't know. I don't even know if it was a patient. All Sholto told me of the event itself was that it took place in New York, and that Patient Zero had contaminated twenty-eight people. One of those twenty-eight had been chased to the mall. Who exactly she was, where she was trying to reach, and who was chasing her, Sholto didn't say. I'm not sure he knew. Of the other twenty-seven, they had gone on to infect people from all walks of life, but it was the airline pilots and politicians with easy access to air travel that spread the infection out of the state and beyond the borders of the U.S. Some turned at the airports, others when boarding, some when they were in transit, some not until they had reached their destination.

I told Jen what I knew, but she didn't seem to care. I suppose she's right, what does it matter?

As the outbreak spread, it became clear that this wasn't a localised problem, or even one that would stay on the other side of the Atlantic. That was when the focus of the news shifted. It happened overnight, literally, as the news outlets were nationalised. They kept their individual tone and format, but they all toed the official line. The UK was free of infection. Britain was safe.

Safe, there's a hollow ring to that word now. It was safe only when compared to the rest of the world. Our first major outbreak occurred four days after New York, but it was quickly dealt with, and news of it suppressed. The number of daily incidents, like the calls to the police about strange noises from an unlit house, or the isolated cases of boats running aground, stayed in double digits. Without a mobile phone network, with more and more websites failing, the few people who discovered the truth had no way to disseminate it.

I'd been unconscious during the closure of supermarkets and petrol stations, the implementation of the Food Distribution Plan, the press nationalisation, the curfew, martial law, the riots, and the shootings that followed. By the time I woke, order had been restored and a defence plan was in place. Everyone was instructed to stay at home and listen to the official announcements. They were told there were no cases of infection reported in the UK. They were told the government was in control. Yeah, right. Jen was the government, and I've never seen her so scared as she was in the hospital.

12:00, 13th March

I thought I heard a car. If it was, it didn't come close enough for me to see it. It did sound like an engine, though. Perhaps I'm imagining it, hearing a phantom sound because I want that car to arrive. I know it's coming and I don't want to miss it. I can't miss it. I've got to be ready. My phone's on. There's no signal, but that doesn't seem to matter. There was no signal when the last message came in. The battery is down to fifty percent. That could be a problem. I didn't have it plugged in since the day before yesterday so that means about forty-eight hours of battery remaining. I'll turn it off. It's best to be cautious.

I have to keep moving around. I'd prefer to sit on the bed, next to the window, with my back against the wall. That way I can see outside, and rest my leg at the same time. Every half hour or so, the muscles start to cramp. Perhaps it's something to do with blood flow. I wish I knew. If only I had the internet. Not the internet I had over the last few weeks, no, not the one which took twenty minutes to load a page, I mean the proper internet.

Since the outbreak, I've spent a lot of time sitting here by the window, watching. At first I saw people skulking away in the middle of the night. Then there was the evacuation when people went by in droves. Then the undead started to appear. At first, it was just one or two. They ambled slowly down the street with that slow gait I'd call a stroll if it wasn't for the bloody stains on their clothing. Over the past few days They've stopped moving on. Now They just stand in a weird sort of half squat, half crouch. It's like They're waiting for something, and I just sit and watch for any kind of movement, any indication that They know I'm here.

Last night, I couldn't sleep. I knew the undead were there, outside in the dark, but I couldn't see Them. It was the worst night of my life, but I know tonight will be worse.

I've not much of a view. The house is built on a corner with a slight elevation. From up here in the attic, I can see the rooftops for this street and the next. Below the roofs, I can count sixty windows, most of which belong to flats. Below that is a hundred-yard stretch of road.

I inherited the house three years ago from an uncle I barely knew. He'd been halfway and a million pounds into renovating the place. When I say halfway, I mean the place had been gutted and half the floors were ripped up. He'd been an investor in the firm Jen and I set up. What I didn't realise until after he'd died was that he'd bought the house in the company's name, saddling me very neatly with the mortgage. I had to give up my flat in Pimlico and move in, converting the downstairs into four apartments with money I borrowed from Jen's parents.

My flat in Pimlico was spectacular. It had an open-plan sitting room and kitchen, an office, a proper walk-in shower, and a bedroom big enough to fit an emperor-size bed, all within a ten-minute saunter of Westminster. Now my entire living space would fit in my old bedroom with space to spare.

My uncle lived up here. It was the only part of the house he'd finished before his death. He was the one who'd put in the balcony and fitted the glass doors so there'd be enough natural light for him to paint his watercolours. I had the glass tinted after a very polite letter from a neighbour pointed out that my morning walk from bed to the shower left nothing to the imagination.

13:10, 13th March

I thought I heard a car again. I'm sure it was a car, but there are so many houses to deflect the sound, it could be anywhere within a mile of here. In the summer, if I left the balcony doors open at night, I could hear goods trains rattling by, and the railway has to be at least half a mile away. Now those sounds are gone. There's nothing but the quiet rustling of wind, and the erratic shuffling of undead feet.

I don't know if the zombies would see me if I stood in front of the balcony's glass doors. I don't want to risk it, so I'll sit on the bed, waiting for my leg to cramp up.

I tried the phone again, just in case, but there was no answer. Perhaps the phone's broken. It *must* be broken. Jen would know her driver didn't come back, wouldn't she? Of course she would. She'll send someone else, but I've got to be patient. She's got millions of evacuees to feed and house. She knows where I am. I've just got to be patient.

My four tenants moved out with the first wave of evacuees. That was on the 6th March, after Jen's television broadcast announcing that the evacuation would begin on the 7th. In that same broadcast, she revealed that the vaccine was ready, but it would only be distributed to evacuees when they reached the muster points.

A few hours before the broadcast, Jen had brought me my last care package. I suppose I was so caught up in the excitement of new food and, later, by the sight of all those evacuees trudging down the road outside, that I didn't notice my tenants were gone until the following morning. Traffic, trains, aeroplanes, kettles boiling, cups rattling, cupboard doors closing. All those little audible cues that you've woken to an ordinary world, they were all gone.

Around mid-morning, I finally mustered the courage to go downstairs and confirm I was alone. It took an age to get down to the first floor. I can't remember the last time I had to lift anything close to my own weight. Probably not since school, and maybe not even then. I tried lowering my good leg first and taking the weight on the crutches, but the stairs are too steep and narrow for that. Instead, it was crutches first, then I had to contort my body into an L-shape at each step. It was agony. I almost gave up after the third step.

The two first-floor flats were empty. The keys were left in the locks. There wasn't even a note. I haven't checked the ground-floor flats. I did try calling out, but as it took all of my energy to get down one flight of stairs, I didn't bother going any further. Besides, what would be the point? I've got food and Jen will send another car. Probably, in all the confusion of the evacuation, she's not realised that the car hasn't returned, but soon she'll ask someone, they'll check, and then they'll send somebody. I've just got to be patient.

14:40, 13th March

When Jen visited that last time, she didn't stay long. Her security people were nervous, and wanted her to hurry up and leave. It wasn't that they actually said "Hand over the food, and let's get out of here," but you could tell they wanted to be elsewhere. One of them stuck to her side the whole time. It's not that we needed privacy, our relationship was never in that particular place, but the soldier followed her in and watched her the whole time she was here.

This was after the prime minister's disappearance. According to Jen, he'd had a breakdown, and been temporarily replaced by Sir Michael Quigley, the foreign secretary. According to Sholto, the PM had been forcibly removed during what in other times would be described as a coup.

19

Jen didn't say where she was going. She didn't say much at all, but as she was leaving, she asked me to wish her luck. The only other time she'd said that was the night before the by-election. I was still furious with her for abandoning our company for the security of a government paycheck, but I wished her luck anyway. It's what you do. So as she left my flat, I said good luck and tried to smile like I meant it.

It's the other soldier who's down in the street. I never spoke to him, never knew his name, but he's the one who died coming to rescue me.

16:00, 13th March

There's no power. There's still water, but without electricity there'll be no more hot showers. Fortunately, that's not a great hardship since it was a pain trying to wash in that small cubicle. I had to sit on a stool underneath the showerhead with the cast wrapped in a bin-liner. The shower's such a small space, I had to leave the door open, and so the bedroom carpet got soaked. I know, who cares about the carpet in times like these? But it's my carpet, my house, and as much as I sometimes hate it, my *home*. I suppose that attitude is the same one that compelled so many refugees to leave with bicycles and trolleys weighed down with far more than they could carry. It's a refusal to accept that the world's changed.

No power for the kettle, though. That's a real blow. I'd begun to ritualise making tea. Waiting for the kettle to boil, and then for the tea to brew meant a few minutes in which I could ignore the nightmare outside. I don't have any milk, not real milk, though Jen left some of the powdered kind. No, there's been no real milk since before I went into hospital. Of course, since the fridge no longer works, there would be no way of keeping it fresh. No fridge. Not that there was much in there. What little there was went off while I was in hospital. I didn't do much cooking. Sandwiches were about the extent of my culinary expertise. Ready-meals were for when I felt extravagant. Usually I ate out, never anywhere particularly grand, but it was better to spend a few extra quid each day than have all my clothes smell of cooking. No more fry-ups. I have an electric stove, a two-ring affair on top of the world's smallest oven. Even if it was gas it wouldn't matter; that was shut off the morning of the evacuation.

Today's lesson? You really can't make tea with cold water. In the same way I know the sun's a long way away, I knew that tea has to be made with boiling water, but I'd never tried it before. I tried making coffee with cold water, but the granules didn't dissolve. Maybe they would with some other brand, but not with the stale jar I've got.

No more bread maker. I used to set the timer so there would be a fresh loaf when I got home. Oh, the smell of fresh bread... It was wonderful coming home to that smell. I've still got the flour, about half a kilo, but like I said, it's an electric oven.

No films, TV, or music, but I can live without those. I never had much time for television and definitely no time for the cinema. As for music, I rated it on its ability to block out the sound from outside, not on any artistic merit. I regret that now.

There's no heating. It's a small room, but it's a big, draughty house, and I'm well aware that I'm the only thing radiating heat in here. Technically, it's spring, but it still feels like winter. At least there's been no snow since the end of January.

If the power's out in London, how long will it be before the water is cut off?

Chin up, be positive, each day will be warmer than the last, and there's always the radio. It's a wind-up thing with a solar panel on the top. It was another Christmas present from Jen, a private joke after I missed the opening segment on a talk show I was on. I thought they were talking about TB in badgers, but they'd moved onto the MMR jab, so when I started talking about culling... well, the station got a lot of calls that day.

The solar panel never worked, and I have to wind the crank for an hour to give the radio's battery thirty minutes of charge. Usually it's plugged into the mains. Keeping it running is now my principal form of exercise. Since the evacuation, all they've broadcast is "Listen for Announcements" followed by the dreariest choral music ever recorded. I think it's on an automated loop. Even before the evacuation, it wasn't much better. After the first twenty-four hours, the TV and radio went back to almost normal programming. They still had updates in the news bulletins, but by that stage, and whether they believed them or not, I think all anyone cared about were those few words at the beginning "There are no reported outbreaks in the UK". For the rest of the time it was music on the radio and old sitcoms, World War Two movies, and sports on the television.

There was a lot of sport on television during the fortnight before the evacuation. They'd shut the stadiums, but the matches were played anyway. With the pubs closed it kept people indoors. I watched about ten minutes of the West Ham versus Arsenal match. The stands were empty, and without the sound of a crowd, the game seemed vapid and pointless, despite the goals.

They considered broadcasting President Grant Maxwell's address as a way of filling time. I'm glad they didn't. It was timed to go out exactly a week after the outbreak in New York. By then, I'm not sure how many people in America were left, or able, to watch. In the U.S., the official line was that the crisis was under control. The reality was that America had already collapsed. Millions had fled the cities in search of a safe haven, and the infection had gone with them.

President Maxwell shouldn't have given the broadcast. He certainly shouldn't have done it from the lawn of the White House. Someone persuaded him that it was essential, that it would calm the populace and restore faith in his government and his leadership. Since he only took the oath of office in January, I'm not sure how much faith anyone had in his leadership. But that was why the speech had to be made, and why it had to be made in front of the White House. Public and politicians, in America and across the world, had to see that he was still in Washington, still fighting the good fight. He had to appear in control.

The speech itself wasn't spectacular. It wasn't moving. It had none of the oratorical skill that had won him November's election. It was just a string of words for the president to say while the cameras focused on the West Wing staffers arrayed in ranks behind and to either side. The visual of a president and his staff still there, still working, was spoiled by the Marines deployed as if they were guarding prisoners. After what happened, it hardly matters.

The president was nearing the end of his speech. He'd just said "God bless you, and God—" He stopped right in the middle of the sentence, and it sounded like he'd just sworn. The cameras stayed on him. For a long few seconds, the president stared slack-jawed into the lens. In the background came a scream. There was a flurry of gunshots, more screaming, more gunshots, and the feed was finally cut. The picture returned to a studio where a presenter blithely continued with announcements about water purification and energy conservation, as if anyone who saw it could pretend that they didn't know what had just happened.

There was another camera, one belonging to a group of students from the University of Notre Dame. They'd been filming a documentary on the inner workings of government. It was intended as part of a get-out-the-vote effort aimed at teenagers who'd be old enough to vote in the midterms. The students had been shadowing the politicians since before the inauguration. After the outbreak, with so much else going on, no one thought to take away their credentials. They just kept recording and uploading the raw footage, but not to the Net. They knew that if it became public, they'd lose their access. Instead, they sent it to the one person with whom they thought it would be safe: Sholto. He forwarded it to me along with a copy of the footage the networks broadcast. From the two sets of video, I've pieced together what happened.

A staffer had been infected, died, and turned in a bathroom just inside the security cordon. How she'd been infected, I don't know. After the lockdown, and after President Maxwell announced he was staying in D.C., the staff had slept at their desks. During the broadcast, since everyone was outside and looking either at the president or at the cameras, and since the zombie was wearing a suit with a pass hanging round its neck, no one realised it was undead until it lunged at the crowd.

The Secret Service reacted with precision and speed, and in accordance with decades of training. They aimed for the centre mass. The zombie must have been hit at least thirty times. It spun. It fell. It got up. The agents changed their aim. The zombie's head exploded as it was

23

simultaneously struck by dozens of bullets. When the camera refocused on the podium a mere fifteen seconds later, the president had gone, his exit marking the end of the federal government. And now, though I watched that clip a dozen times before the power went out, I couldn't tell you a single word the president said.

18:00, 13th March

I've filled all the containers I could find with water in case that gets turned off, too. Getting into the kitchen wasn't fun. I really *hate* crutches. It took about five times longer than it normally would just to fill the measuring jug. I've also filled the saucepans, the kettle, and a couple of vases I keep for when I'm showing new tenants around. In total I have about twenty pints. I know because I used the measuring jug to fill everything. It took longer that way, but that's about all the weight I could lift while bent precariously over the sink. It's not much of a reserve, but I don't have enough space in here to store any more. Even if I did, I don't have any other containers in which I could put the water.

Twenty pints. That's about ten litres. I once read that they got by on a pint of water a day in the desert during the war. If the water's cut off, I have twenty days.

18:50, 13th March

To have a cup of tea, or not to have a cup of tea, that is this evening's question. In order to have one, I'll need to boil water. To do that, I need a fire. Two of the flats downstairs have working chimneys. There's enough furniture and, Bradbury forgive me, books to get a blaze going, but what about the smoke? Will the zombies see it? Will They smell it?

Jen left a few extra boxes of tea, which was kind of her, but now I wish she'd brought more food. I think the food came from her flat. That would explain why the packages are mismatched. She used to like being seen at the supermarket, and the press liked printing photographs of her shopping basket. It was a way of boosting her name recognition, and proving to the electorate that she really did know the price of a pint of milk.

Would a fire attract the undead? I don't think so. I can count three plumes of smoke in the distance, but maybe those are too far away for the zombies outside to notice. I don't really need a cup of tea. No, it's too great a risk.

When I went downstairs to look for my tenants, I didn't spend long in their rooms, but I did spot Jezzelle's books. There were three long shelves running the length of the wall. The top two shelves were given over to romantic fantasy. Not what I'm in the mood for, at all. The final row was nothing but zombie fiction. I brought a couple up here. Why not? I thought there might be something useful in one of them. It wasn't as if it could hurt.

They had the zombie people on the TV. Experts, they called them. They'd start the interview with something like "Now we're joined by John Smith, author of 'Twenty Ways to Survive a Zombie Attack'. John, welcome, now what should we be doing?"

I can't believe they actually broadcast things like that. I mean, I know it was just the media's knees jerking in the only way they knew how, but did they really think this would do more good than harm? Or was it that they were stuck in that old mindset, that if they didn't fill the airtime, viewers would switch to one of their competitors. Without any real experts to ask, who better than a bunch of fictionauts who'd never faced anything more dangerous than a looming deadline? Of course, what made it worse was that anyone, author, scientist, retired four-star general, anyone who had even an ounce of truly useful experience had either fled to the hills or bunkered down, and was definitely not appearing on television. So, instead, they got the people who really, genuinely had nothing useful to say. Like the one who said you should retreat to the top floor and break down the staircase, that way if the undead got into the house, you would be safe upstairs. Brilliant! How exactly do you get out of the house when you run out of food and water? What if there's a fire? This farrago only lasted until the press was nationalised, but you'd think they could have come up with something more helpful to broadcast.

Anyway, I digress. My conclusion is that I really hate zombie books. I didn't read them properly. Who'd want to, with the real undead right outside? But I flicked through them again this afternoon to see if there was any practical advice I'd missed. A couple of them did offer step-by-step instructions on how to clean and maintain an M16, but nothing about how long it takes water to stagnate.

The doctor said I'd need a cast for three to four months. She also said I'd need to come back in a week for more x-rays. They wanted to check how my leg was healing, and make sure the bones were properly aligned and knitting together. She said the cast was temporary until… then she trailed off and looked at Jen's two bodyguards. I never did get those x-rays, or a more permanent cast. I'll get a new cast when I get out of London. I hope I will. With so many evacuees, the enclaves' medical facilities will be stretched thin. They might even have run out of supplies. Well, I'll worry about that when I get there.

I've decided the cast should stay on for another eleven weeks, that's seventy-seven days. At which point, if I haven't been able to get one of those fibreglass things the celebs get, I'm going to rip the damn thing off and ceremonially burn it. For now, I'll keep the containers filled, change the water every day, and worry about the rest when it stops coming out of the taps. It's getting dark now, too dark to write. I'll just sit up and wait for the stars. Seventy-seven days to go.

Day 2, 76 days to go

10:00, 14th March

I got up at dawn, but was awake long before then. After thirty-three years of sleeping on my side, sleeping on my back doesn't come easily, and my broken leg makes it next to impossible. Every time I drifted towards sleep, I'd forget about the leg, try rolling over, and find the immovable mass of the cast anchoring me to the bed. That woke me up, and the process would start again. Besides, it's hard to sleep while the water tank is gurgling a few inches from your head.

That's right, the water tank. It supplies the hot water for the two flats with baths. Or it did. The point is that there's a tank filled with water a few inches of plyboard away. When I realised that, at around four this morning, I felt relieved, almost calm. Now, I'm fully aware that having ones spirits buoyed by something so trivial is indicative of how desperate my situation is, but I don't care. I'll take any glimmer of hope I can find.

My morning ablutions took about an hour. I can't get the desk chair into the bathroom, so I have to walk in backwards, supporting my weight on the crutches while lowering myself onto the toilet, and... well, okay, you don't need a picture. It takes a long time, that's my point. Breakfast didn't. This morning, I had a tin of peaches and a long stare at my box of tea.

I guess because of that, since about seven a.m., I've been making lists. It's not something I'd usually spend time on, but what else is there to do? I started with a list of things I wish I had, like a torch. What I'd really like is a helicopter and an extraction team, but I'd settle for a torch. If I had one, I'd be able to read at night. I'd have to do it in the bathroom, sitting on the toilet with the door closed, because I'm not going to risk Them noticing a light. Even so, a night in the cramped bathroom would be infinitely preferable to one staring at the ceiling in the dark.

The next thing I wrote on the list was hot water. A torch and hot water. The first may be downstairs, the second definitely is, or at least the fireplaces are.

Going downstairs scares me. I'm not ashamed to admit it. I'm scared, and it's not some nameless fear of the unknown, it's a fear of slipping on the stairs and breaking my other leg; of being woken in the middle of the night by the sound of the front door breaking; of being trapped up here with the undead on the stairs outside, left with nothing but a choice between starvation and suicide.

I didn't check the front door. I think it's closed, but I can't be certain. There were a few times when I got home at some ungodly hour to find the front door open. It sticks a bit and needs to be lifted closed. As they didn't bother telling me they were leaving, what are the chances my tenants shut the door when they left? Do I go downstairs? I'll have to eventually, but if the door is open and if a zombie's inside, can I deal with it? I'm safe here. Safe until the car comes. Then what? There are over twenty of Them in the street now. How many people will Jen send? Last time she just sent the one guy, what if next time she only sends one? What if he waits in the street? I can't expect him to kill twenty zombies, climb up the stairs, carry me down, and deal with a threat in the house as well. When the car comes I've got to be ready to meet it. And what if he can't deal with all twenty of Them? What if he runs to the house, seeking shelter, only to find a locked door in front and the undead following behind? That settles it. I'm going downstairs.

15:30, 14ᵗʰ March

I've never looted before. It was rather fun. I've returned with a half-kilo bag of sugar, a torch, and another ten zombie books. I've been more selective this time, picking those most likely to contain some vaguely applicable survival tips. One got four stars from *Survivalist Quarterly*. I wonder if that's out of five or ten.

Before I went downstairs, I had to find a weapon. That's another thing I've never done before. I've never needed to, nor thought I'd ever have to. The best I could find was the out-sized metal-handled hammer I bought a year ago in a moment of desperation. I needed to put down a carpet to hide the disturbing stains a newly ex-tenant had left on the polished wooden floor. It was the only hammer in the only open hardware shop I could find. Too heavy for the task, it left a series of quarter-inch dents around each of the tacks. It's a far cry from the machetes and shotguns that feature in these books. Fortunately, I didn't have to use it.

I couldn't bring much back upstairs. Sadly that's not a problem because my tenants took most of the obviously useful items with them.

Tom and Jezzelle had the smaller two-room flats. Each has a modest bedroom, bathroom, and a living-room-kitchen with a working fireplace. They're not huge rooms, but they were reasonably priced, and far bigger than the space I live in. Tom's from Macau, on a two-year postgraduate archaeology placement at UCL. He seemed like a nice enough guy, though I didn't see much of him.

As a rule, I kept away from the tenants, partly because I was the landlord, and partly because I didn't want to hear, see, or know anything that someone working at Whitehall shouldn't. Tom made that easy by spending most of his time away on digs, or on secondment to other universities. At least that was what it said in the emails he sent letting me know he'd be away. I didn't find much in his room beyond some textbooks on ancient cultures, some others in Mandarin, a massive collection of DVDs, and the usual bric-a-brac we all collect. Almost none of it is of any use.

Almost. I said almost. He had a flashlight made of red and blue plastic with 'The Man of Steel' printed on the handle. It's either a cheap kids' toy or a geek's very expensive collectable, which I guess is why he left it behind. He was used to camping out in the middle of nowhere, so he probably had a very good field kit with a very good torch, and he took it with him. As for this one, it would be useless outside, but for reading at night, it's perfect.

In the kitchen was the half bag of sugar, a few tins, a pack of dried apricots, and some herbs and spices. I assume they're herbs and spices. They're in little bags stamped with Chinese writing. I'm pretty sure one of them is oregano. Probably.

As for Jezzelle's flat, well, the biggest discovery was that she repainted the bedroom a garish purple. I definitely didn't give her permission to do that, which I suppose is why she didn't tell me. As for her possessions, they were mostly clothes, costume jewellery, and bath salts. Oh, and I discovered her real name is Jessica. I wonder why she didn't use it.

I decided not to light the fire, not tonight. It's getting late, and there's a limited amount of fuel inside. The coal is in the shed outside. The tenants had a coalscuttle, key, and the right to take however much they wanted. Wish I'd known how cold the winters were going to get when I wrote the contract. Outside, there's three sacks, but outside might as well be Newcastle. Inside I've got two scuttles, each less than half full. That's enough fuel for about four fires.

I laid the fireplace in Tom's room, so I'm prepared. I prefer his room, less clutter, less purple. Then I brought my haul up here. All in all, a good day.

17:00, 14th March

I forgot to check the doors.

18:00, 14th March

That wasn't fun. The first time I went downstairs today, it was an expedition, an escape. I'd been so distracted by the simple joy of a change of environment that I'd forgotten why I'd gone down there in the first place. Stupid! Stupid! Stupid! Oh, how I wish I dared scream.

Crutch in hand, hammer tucked into my belt, I went back downstairs. Those last few steps were the worst. Sitting down, sliding forward, bracing my good leg, lowering myself onto the next step while straining not to let the cast bang on the staircase. Each agonising inch took me further into the dark shadows. My leg got heavier until it was a burning, impossible weight. I tried to be silent, but the harder I tried, the more noise I seemed to make. Each creak of the stairs, each thud of the cast, each ragged, heaving breath seemed amplified tenfold.

The doors *were* closed. As quietly as I could, I slid across the deadbolts. It'll slow me down when rescue arrives, but I won't need to worry about noise then.

I *do* feel safer now, almost calm. Almost. My heart's still thumping away, but that's probably the adrenaline. The doors to the ground-floor flats are locked, so are the front and back doors. I had to double-check the upstairs flats. I mean, I knew no one was in there, but I had to check anyway. Does that count as paranoia, or caution? Either way, it's got to be healthy.

Day 3, 75 days to go

09:00, 15th March

There's one out there walking along the road slightly faster than the others. It's moving at an easy two or three miles an hour, almost as if it was heading off on its morning commute. Not that it's dressed for that. It's wearing thick trousers tucked into socks, sturdy boots, and a thick jacket that's torn and stained brown around the shoulders. It's even wearing a backpack. I wonder if it was going to join the evacuation, but changed its mind, thinking it'd be safer on its own, so turned back, maybe heading home, only to end up as the thing it had wanted to avoid.

Just then it stopped, turned, and looked about, almost as if it had heard something. It's crossing the street, angling towards a house at the far end of the road. It's walking faster now, almost with that same determined speed I've seen when They are about to attack. It's stopped.

It's been standing there for about twenty minutes now, and its head is turning slowly from side to side. Is it looking around? Can it see? Or can it hear something, but can't pinpoint the sound?

11:00, 15th March

I'm bored. Bored and hungry. The hiker is still standing there, motionless except for its head, which slowly shifts from side to side. Why it's doing that, I can't tell. Watching it is about a notch more interesting than daytime TV, and a notch below watching paint dry. Isn't there a saying that fear breeds boredom, or is it the other way around? Well, either way, it's true.

Dinner last night was a cold tin of beans. I hate beans. I've always hated them. Jen knows I hate them. She used to taunt me with them when we were kids. She didn't like them much either, but she'd always ask for extra. When her parents weren't looking, she'd take a big spoonful and hold it just over my plate, silently threatening to drop it. We spent a lot of time together when we were younger. Her father had known my parents before they died. I think it was her father, not my uncle, who paid for my

31

schooling, though I never dared ask. Anyway, that's why I think the food had to come from her flat. If it was from a government storeroom, and she had her choice of what to include, she wouldn't have brought me beans.

I was thinking about stringing together a bunch of empty cans and sticking them halfway down the stairs as a sort of early warning device. I don't think They will be able to get through the front doors, but the ground-floor windows would be easy enough to break. Would the sound of rattling tins attract more of Them? I think I could deal with one if it was alone. Yes, I could manage that, but what if there were two, or three? I suppose if They smashed a window, I'd hear the sound of breaking glass. I would, wouldn't I?

17:00, 15th March

I wonder where the car was going to take me. Not to one of the muster points. That's what we called the temporary evacuation centres. There, people would be physically examined, given the vaccine, and sent onward to an island or enclave. When Jen said a car was coming for me, I asked if I was being evacuated. She said no. She was going to send me somewhere safe. Her reply came by text message. Since leaving the hospital, a lot of our communication was by text. I asked her whether I could get a permit for a ticket on one of the trains leaving London during the week before the evacuation. My broken leg meant I was entitled, but she said no to that, too. At the time, and after a little thought, I decided I was grateful. Of all the places I didn't want to be, in an evacuee centre with tens of thousands of others was near the top of the list. Now, though, it seems preferable to being stuck here, alone in south London.

The muster points will all be closed now. They were only meant to be open for twenty-four hours, at least that's what people were told. Because of the sheer number of evacuees, it was always going to take longer than that. It was hoped the evacuation could be completed in twenty-four hours, but they planned for forty-eight. After that, the muster points were going to be shut.

Perhaps the car was going to take me to a bunker. Perhaps to one of those decommissioned Cold War refuges that were refurbished in the panic at the beginning of the millennium. Perhaps I'd have ended up on a cot next to the Windsors. I don't think I'd have enjoyed that any more than they would.

19:00, 15th March

It's seventy-five days until the cast can come off. It's forty days until the food runs out.

Day 4, 74 days to go

07:00, 16th March

I can see twenty-two of Them from the window. That's two more than yesterday. I think. I'm not sure. There's one wearing a blue jacket that I might have seen before, except then it had a hat. It was one of those cheap pork-pie hats that everyone seemed to wear last year. Today there's no hat, not on it, or any of the others. So did the hat fall off, or is it a different zombie?

I need to keep a more accurate count. Jen might call before sending a car, and she'll want to know how many zombies are here. Assuming a roughly equal distribution around the entire house, there are between sixty and seventy within shouting distance. That seems like a lot.

It can't be like this everywhere, can it? Surely not after the evacuation, not if… unless… it would mean that about half the country's population was out on the streets, and that can't be right. The only other explanation is that the undead are gathering here for some reason. No, not gathering, that suggests intelligence. Drawn, perhaps? But if They are being drawn here, then by what?

They don't seem to move much. They just squat on their haunches, almost as if They're waiting, but that's what humans do and They are not human.

No. They're not human.

09:10, 16th March

I'm sitting extra quietly. I know that sounds childish, but it's possible I'm making more noise than I realise, and that's somehow summoning Them here. So I'm sitting extra quietly, just to see what happens outside. And, since we're being childish, what do you do when you're sitting quietly? You read.

The zombie books are useless, but I bet you guessed that. Okay, not completely useless but not exactly helpful. Reading them gave me something to do last night, right up until the battery died, but any advice even approaching the practical starts with the assumption that a) you're mobile; b) you're armed; c) you live in a fictional world where your survival is guaranteed, at least until the last few pages.

Three of the ten I picked up yesterday, including the one with the promising *Survivalist Quarterly* review, involved the protagonist discovering a house belonging to a Mormon family which was stocked with a year's supply of food. At no point did it give any advice on how to spot a house that belonged to Mormons. I think there was a large community of them near Bath, or Boston, or Buxton, or somewhere beginning with B, but that's about as useful as saying they're in Utah. Were there other communities with that sort of cultural preparedness built in? I don't know. Like I said, not helpful.

There was one book, just as useless as the others, but which I actually enjoyed reading. It's not a survival book, but a comic re-working of Romeo and Juliet, telling the story of unattainable love through the romance of a zombie and a human. The Juliet character had a pet dog whose sacrifice became the pivotal moment in the final chapter. I just can't stop thinking about it.

Down in the street, there's a woman I vaguely recognise. She lived in a house on the next road. I've no idea what her name is. After all, this is London; no one talks to their neighbours here. I'd sometimes see her in the park, or occasionally out in the street. We'd nod and smile at one another, and that was that. No words were ever exchanged. Now she's just another zombie.

During the last couple of years, I couldn't afford gym membership, not with the millstone mortgage around my neck, so I took up running. Not that frequently. It was more out of guilt when I'd wake on a Saturday morning and realise I'd done nothing more physical than lift a coffee mug during the previous week. I'd drag on my trainers and head to the park before my brain had a chance to convince my body that going back to sleep would be a far better idea. That's when I'd see her, running the same circuit as me.

She always had a little dog with her, a tiny thing with stubby legs, big hair, and either a coat or a bow depending upon the season. She'd start at a walk, just meandering along, talking to the dog, encouraging it. After a few dozen yards, she would stop talking as the walk became brisk, then a jog, then a run, but the dog couldn't keep up. The woman wasn't cruel, just forgetful. For a few feet, the dog would be dragged along. The woman would finally remember, stop, bend down and apologise, stroking and soothing her pet. Then they would start walking again at that slow sedate pace. As sure as the sun rises, after a few dozen yards, she'd speed up until the dog was being pulled along.

Maybe she ran out of food. Maybe she thought the longer she waited, the worse things would get. Maybe she thought she was truly on her own. I'm inclined to think it's the latter because she made her move on the 11th, the day after the car came to collect me. The sight of a dead soldier left in the street must have made her think no more help was coming, not here anyway.

I watched it all happen. Wearing a backpack and hefting a cricket bat, she stormed through the back gate to her house, and charged towards her car. She knocked two zombies over on her way there, but from my vantage point I could see They were still moving, twitching and crawling after her. The bag went into the car and she followed it. The engine wouldn't start. She didn't panic. I was impressed with that. She got out, looked around, and saw that there was a zombie between her and the house. Realising it would be on her in seconds, she turned, and walked briskly up the road.

The other zombies in the street had noticed her by then. Two of the closest, their faces too disfigured to even guess at their gender, slouched towards her. She gripped the bat tightly in both hands and scythed it forward. She misjudged the blow. It barely grazed the first and missed the second completely. She swung again. This time, one of Them went down. She pivoted gracefully, shifting her weight to her back foot, and brought the bat down with a ferocious backhand. The creature's skull shattered, and I swear I saw teeth fly out of its mouth. It was stunning, and I guess she thought so too because she stopped. It was only for the merest heartbeat, just long enough to adjust her grip, to take a breath. It was long enough for the first zombie, the one who'd been crawling along the kerb, to rise up and bite her leg. She screamed, and brought the bat down again and again until its head was nothing but a reddish-brown smear on the pavement. By then, she was surrounded. I didn't watch the rest.

She lost an arm at some point, chewed off above the shoulder. So much of her left calf is gone that she can't really stand. She just half sits, half lies on the pavement, occasionally dragging herself a few feet to the left, and then to the right, leaving a terrible stain behind her.

I wonder what her name was. I wonder what happened to her dog.

11:00, 16th March

Should I try to get the bag my neighbour took to her car? Relatively speaking, it's not far away, but is it worth the risk? I can't decide if there's likely to be anything useful in it. Not weapons, clearly, since if she had anything better than a cricket bat she would have used it. Maybe there's food. Then again, she left the bag in the car, so maybe not.

I have to accept some responsibility for her death. No, not responsibility, that's not quite the right word. I didn't know she was there, nor did she know I was here, but her actions were precipitated by the car pulling up and Jen's bodyguard being killed. If I wasn't here then maybe she'd still be in her home, maybe she would have lived, if only for a little longer.

No, I shouldn't think like that. I mustn't think like that. Her death is not my responsibility. Even if I'd called out, I doubt I could have reached the door in time to let her in. Even if I had, she'd have ended up in here, with the undead right outside, knowing where we were. I've searched my soul and can't decide if I kept silent out of self-preservation, fear, or cowardice. Whether it was the right thing to do or not, it wasn't a conscious decision but it was a decision, and it's made and done.

It was that book, the romantic idea of two people finding and saving each other, of a zombie with compassion. Reality is just so much more depressing.

But the batteries ran out last night. I need more unless I want to face another night in the dark, so back downstairs I go.

19:00, 16th March

Out of all the job descriptions I've ever had, I think looter sounds the best. It's more proactive than survivor. Certainly, committing what, a month ago, would have been called theft brought me out of my maudlin introspection. I found some more batteries in Jessica's flat. I refuse to call her Jezzelle any longer. I'd apologise, but since she isn't here… There were four batteries in total, but none are new. Hopefully, they'll last the night.

There's still a chance of finding another torch in the downstairs flats, but it's such a supremely practical item, I doubt either of them ever thought of buying one. Those two were both utterly hopeless, completely incapable of changing a light bulb, or even turning off the central heating. The summer before last, when I was at the party conference, I kept getting emails saying the house was too hot. The tenants complained that they'd tried everything, but couldn't fix it. In the end, I got in the car and drove back, arriving about three a.m. I solved the problem ten seconds later by turning the thermostat down.

No, I can't see them having anything useful, but am I any better? I mean, there's my toolkit, but what else of any practical use do I have here? My torch, along with the survival blanket, wrench, multi-tool, and decent pair of walking boots are in the boot of my car in an underground car park on the other side of the river.

When I found out my tenants had gone, I called Jen. I was sure that, since they'd left while the curfew was still in place, they must surely have been arrested and detained. She was in a cabinet meeting and I ended up speaking to an assistant, some officious dogsbody whom I'd never heard of and who clearly hadn't a clue who I was. I was assured that, due to the large number of people who'd left early, no one was being arrested. Then he added that they were "just muddling through with the evacuation as best they could. Thanks for the concern." Then he hung up.

My plan, for it was my plan, though others may have come to the same conclusions, was that an evacuation of our urban areas was the only practical solution to the problems we were about to face. The only other choice was to tell the nation to stay inside, barricade their homes, and hope that the zombies would die or decay before the uninfected starved. Some in the cabinet office wanted to extend that idea and use our nuclear arsenal to destroy those urban areas. That would reduce the pressure on what were increasingly scarce resources, but there was a very real risk it would bring about the anarchy and chaos that was taking grip elsewhere.

Our Thin Blue Line was stretched taut, even bolstered as it was by camouflage green. All that prevented the mass desertions that had spelled the end for Russia was that our troops had nowhere on the entire planet left to flee to. We needed to give people hope, and asking them to stay put was never going to do that.

We had no food imports except that which could be stolen from aid depots and foreign shipping. The refineries were running out of oil to process, and what little fuel we had was being reserved for coastal defence. There were close to thirty million citizens, tourists, and refugees in our cities and urban areas. The situation was dire, and the country on the verge of collapse. The plan I came up with was simple. It had to be.

First, we would move the people to the coast where it would be easier to distribute what we could steal and fish. Then our aim was, or is, I suppose, to begin massive agricultural works. With the sea at our backs, we'll push forward and reclaim the island. It's not the greatest plan, I see that now, but we had so little time.

Six days after New York, the announcement was made that there was to be an evacuation. No date was set and only scant details were given, but following an increase in riots and curfew-breaking, people needed to know that there was a plan and that someone was still governing. The citizens were told to prepare. Those who were physically able had to walk or cycle up to forty miles to a muster point. From there they would be transported to an evacuation zone. Those that couldn't make such a journey would be transported by train or bus.

Each city had its own evacuation plan, with cities subdivided by postcode, each given a different muster point. The bridges over, and the tunnels under, the Thames had been closed, so for London there was a roughly north-south split.

As soon as it was announced, restrictions on travel were increased. Most motorways and many A-roads were closed to the little traffic that was left, and protective fences were erected along the routes the evacuees were going to take. Anyone caught trying to leave a city without a permit was lucky if they ended up working on one of the gangs fortifying the roads.

Not everyone had to stay and wait. The doctors, nurses, scientists, engineers, logisticians, builders, plumbers, electricians, and others whose skills were needed to cater to the basic needs of the tens of millions of refugees were evacuated, along with their families, over that first week.

Then there were those who remained behind. In order to prevent the kind of anarchy seen in Sao Paulo, the appearance of normality had to be preserved. That's why the football matches were shown on TV. It's why the roads were swept, why the dentists stayed open. I'm proud of that last one. I couldn't think of a better way to reassure people that Britain still functioned than by telling everyone to visit the dentist. A lot of people did. It's pretty clear that of all the priorities after the evacuation, dental supplies are going to be very low on the list, and we don't want to worry about the loss of labour during harvest because of tooth decay. I know, this sounds really petty, but by keeping dentists open, by making all treatment free again, by telling people to go now, because they really wouldn't get a chance in the near future, it made the evacuation real. No, it was more than that, it made the idea of life after the evacuation real, too. That kind of hope was just as important in maintaining order as the sight of a whole regiment marching through the streets.

To ensure that none of those workers tried to abandon their posts, we evacuated their families during the first few days. You can call them hostages if you like, but what else were we going to do? Money wasn't worth anything, food was scarce, and the only valuable commodity we had to offer was safety. That first wave found the enclaves were squalid and cramped, nothing at all like the propaganda footage that was being broadcast, but it was safe.

Perhaps it would have been easier if we'd been able to evacuate the cities immediately. A rolling exodus using the trains, spread out over a week or even longer. But we couldn't. When the evacuation was announced, so was the existence of the vaccine and that it would be administered only at the muster points. We had the delivery mechanism, one hundred million single-dose injection pens stockpiled against the pandemic we'd been waiting decades for, but of the vaccine itself, we had nowhere near enough.

During the latter days of the Cold War, after Britain abandoned its biological weapons programs, it kept up its research into a so-called super-vaccine. It was intended to be a drug that would work against any biological agent the USSR could throw at us. It had little early success. When the Iron Curtain came down, the project was only saved from the axe by virtue of being a major employer in a marginal constituency. Over the decades since, under new management and with the country facing new threats, the project was revitalised until, finally, about eight years ago success was reported in agent RL-291 (9XT).

It wasn't completely effective, far from it. In the early trials thirty percent of the test-animals died, forty percent contracted all seven of the viruses, and twenty-five percent contracted at least one. But consistently, in trial after trial, five percent remained free of infection. It was that five percent that made the agent effective enough to be seen as the first step on a long road of research and development that would ultimately see all the world's worst diseases consigned to the history books. Naturally, it would be the British government who would take the credit.

It was about six years ago that I first came across it. I was looking for a cause for Jen to trumpet after her popularity had been tarnished during a misguided head-to-head with the mayor on live TV. Following a tip from Sholto, I'd been investigating a black hole in a particular hospital's budget. I assumed it was just another scam, we'd had so many, and so I started asking questions. That quickly landed me in an underground room at the MOD being interrogated by some very unpleasant men. I promised to ask no more questions, and they promised that if I did… They didn't finish the sentence. In that place, under those circumstances, they didn't have to.

After the outbreak in New York, after I was released from hospital, I asked Jen about the vaccine and whether it would be worth trying it on this infection. Her response wasn't at all what I was expecting. She seemed shocked that I knew about it. I thought they'd have told her about my time in the dungeons of Whitehall. Ah, secrets, what would politics be without them? She said that yes, it had been tested on humans the day before, and it did work. At least, it worked on some patients, but more time was needed to manufacture enough for the entire population.

I don't know how much I should say, even now. I suppose if this is being read by someone other than myself then national secrets no longer matter. From the time I stopped my digging, RL-291 had been refined, redesigned, and improved. When its existence was announced, we said it was 99.9 percent effective, but that was an exaggeration. According to Jen, the vaccine that was to be used at the muster points would, at best, stop transmission of the virus in eight percent of cases. It was a small lie, I suppose, but a necessary one.

By saying that it would be distributed at the muster points first, we kept the cities from emptying. Even with the influx of troops from overseas, if they'd left en masse there's no way we could have stopped people from flocking to the countryside. For over a week people stayed at home. They queued for food, and some queued for the dentists. Above all, they waited.

While Britain waited, the world collapsed. Rioting consumed Europe as those from the Mediterranean countries headed north, towards the illusory security of the cold. Why they thought that would help them I can't say; clearly none of them had seen the footage from Canada. Those from Eastern Europe headed south, apparently seeking food. Great waves of refugees collided all over the continent, unable to find food, shelter, or protection. With them went the infection.

Some military units from the northern coastal regions of Denmark and Germany headed northwest to Greenland, joining elements of the Scandinavian military and refugees from Canada and the northeastern U.S. Others had had the same idea, and this small group, well-armed though they were, was overwhelmed by waves of refugees from across the Americas, all heading for one of the largest coastlines in the world, in a land famous for barren desolation.

China descended into anarchy as the ill-prepared city-dwelling millions headed for the illusory safety of the countryside. North Korea began an artillery barrage of the South after Kim claimed the whole thing was an elaborate U.S. hoax. Having to divide their forces prevented the South Koreans from properly dealing with the infection. By the time the barrage was over, it was an army of the undead marching through the minefields of the DMZ. They reached Pyongyang about the same time as the first waves of the living dead from China waded through the Tumen River.

New Zealand evacuated to the North Island, Australia to Tasmania. Theirs was a more ruthless form of evacuation, taking only a select few of the general population and sinking any ships approaching, whether they came from the mainland or from elsewhere. South Africa tried implementing a similar plan using Madagascar, but they weren't the only ones. That island nation soon descended into a bloody four-way war before the number of infected outnumbered the living, and the war turned into a battle for survival.

Very little of this curtain call of civilisation was broadcast in the UK. Most of what I learned came from Sholto. Or, rather, I culled it from the files he sent. Gigabyte after gigabyte of raw video, audio recordings of calls, satellite images, emails, and pictures. I'm certain he didn't have time to go through it himself. He must have just grabbed all that he could from wherever he could and sent it on. I went through some of it, enough to get an overview, but I thought, and I still do, that there will be enough time in the future to go through it and create a proper archive of the end of our old world.

Almost two weeks after the first scenes were broadcast from New York, when Jen made that final broadcast announcing that the evacuation would start the next day, countries the world over had fallen. All that was left were towns and villages, hamlets and houses, barricaded and held against zombies and refugees alike. They were isolated and alone as the power failed, and that once-mighty global communication system finally collapsed.

For my tenants, the muster point was a golf course near Farningham in Kent. That's about twenty miles from here and further than any Londoner would usually walk in a month, let alone in a day. But what other choice did they have except to stay and starve in the dark?

The roads along the designated routes had been fenced-in and split into lanes. The left lane was for cyclists, the second was for those on foot, the third was for the buses that would collect those who couldn't walk any further. All travel except on the designated fenced-in routes was banned. Those found outside of the evacuation routes would be assumed to be infected, and they would be neutralised.

Once they arrived at the muster point, they would have had a physical examination to check for infection. If they passed, they would be given the vaccine. If they didn't pass the examination... well, you can guess. Those who passed would board a train, bus, coach, or flatbed, and be taken to one of the coastal enclaves being established around fishing towns, ports, power stations, and oil refineries. For my tenants, their final destination would have been Folkestone.

Evacuees could take with them only what they could carry but, as long as they could carry it, no restrictions were placed on their luggage. They were advised to bring blankets and clothing and enough food and water for the journey, but beyond that, nothing was as important as emptying the cities and beginning the slow process of rebuilding.

It was expected that thousands, possibly tens of thousands, would become infected, but those numbers were manageable. The plan would reduce a worst-case scenario from an outbreak of millions that would destroy the country into one that would only require the destruction of a walled town.

It was a slapdash plan, a last resort plan, a great undertaking for that time of dire-most need. It was my plan. The germ of which came as I was wheeled from the hospital to the waiting car, then grew over the next day until I sent the forty-page outline to Jen. And that plan was almost implemented. Almost. People didn't wait until it was the turn for their sector. As soon as the announcement was made, people started appearing in the streets. I watched them go by all day, some on their own, some in small groups, some on foot, some cycling, some pushing their gear on pushchairs, others with nothing bigger than a carrier bag. There were no cars, but even if someone had managed to hoard a few gallons of petrol they wouldn't have been able to drive through the throng. That, I have to assume, is where the problems started.

There should, perhaps, be one or two zombies outside my window, and I shouldn't be here to witness it. The routes and the staggered departures were all designed to get people out safely, without risk of infection. Instead they left before they were meant to, before they were expected to, and before the proper defence mechanisms were put in place. That is what I assume. The evidence of my own eyes tells me that what was meant to happen, and what did, lie far apart.

Evacuees? Refugees would be closer to the mark, I don't think any of them truly realised what they were going to, or what they were leaving behind. Whether they were wearing designer hiking boots or plastic trainers from the supermarket, they were going to spend the foreseeable future digging fields, breaking concrete, or gutting fish. And they, out of all the billions on the planet, they'll be the lucky ones.

Day 5, 73 days to go

00:15, 17ᵗʰ March

It's hard to sleep and I can't concentrate to read. The emergency broadcast went off-air for twenty minutes or so. I'm not sure what that means. Maybe it doesn't mean anything. I'm hiding in the bathroom, journal in one hand, pen in the other, the flashlight held between my teeth and the radio on the floor, volume on low. The door's closed and I've wedged a towel against the gap at the bottom of the frame just for caution's sake.

This is a pitiful way to live.

Today is the fifth day without power, which makes it almost four weeks since New York. How long before undead muscles atrophy and their bodies succumb to decay? Longer than it will take mine. I've forty days of food, at best. That's counting raw ingredients which I've no way of cooking, and it's assuming none of it spoils.

12:00, 17ᵗʰ March

I fell asleep last night counting calories. That's a bad joke, I know, but at times like this are there any other kind? I need to focus more on my survival. That's my new mantra.

Based on splitting the tins and the packets up into rough portion sizes, I've got about forty days' worth of food. Well, thirty-nine now, I suppose. It might last longer since I'm not exactly exerting myself. It might be less, because some might spoil. Either way there's a problem with the arithmetic. I've seventy-three days until the cast is due to come off. Then I've got to get the muscles back into working order. Call that another month, and that makes about one hundred days before I can walk close to normally. I'm going to starve long before then.

Jen didn't leave any of the vaccine in her last care package. I guess she knew she'd be sending someone for me. I wonder if there's any in the car.

19:00, 17ᵗʰ March

I spent the afternoon investigating the two ground-floor flats. My hope, my fantasy, was that one of my tenants had bought a box of freeze-dried ready meals and forgotten about it. No such luck.

Getting down the stairs exhausted me. I had to rest at the bottom for a good twenty minutes before I was ready to continue. The first stop was Grace's flat. She was a golfer who didn't quite make it, and earned her living working in the clubhouse at a course on the other side of London. First, I checked the windows were locked and the curtains were closed, then I investigated the bathroom. I wanted to empty the water tank, since it's not been used for over a week. I thought it a good idea to periodically freshen it up. That's when I noticed there wasn't a plug. I can't imagine she'd have taken it with her, so assume she'd lost it. All that was there was an empty chain, dangling forlornly. I tried the shower, but the head was so caked in limescale, only the thinnest trickle of water came out. It's baffling. Where did she wash? Why didn't she say something?

Her cupboards were pretty bare. I found a few more herbs to brighten up my boiled rice, and a few more sets of batteries, but beyond that there was nothing I could see an immediate use for. What was even stranger was the complete absence of golf clubs. I mean, I asked her about that once, about a year after she'd moved in; she'd said that they were kept at the driving range, but I'm starting to wonder.

Juan's was a little more promising. He was an aspiring actor who might have made it one day. His kitchen was worthy of the name. Lots of flour, pulses, sugar, baking powder, spices, and the like. If I had an oven, I'd be fine.

And books! He had books. Lots and lots of books, none of which have anything to do with zombies! And yes, from where I sit that is worthy of an exclamation mark. From the way they were organised, he must have bought them as background reading to parts he was auditioning for. There are lots of travelogues, local and regional histories, true crime books, and biographies of writers and actors. They're the sort of diverting books I'd love to have read on the beach sometime. I brought up a selection. I'm sure I can imagine the beach.

The problem lay in getting my haul up the stairs. The real problem was getting *me* up the stairs, but there's no easy solution to that. I cut one of Juan's sheets into long strips, then twisted and tied them together into an impromptu rope. It wouldn't take my weight, but with one end tied around my belt, the other around the bag, I made my way back upstairs, pulling my haul up afterwards.

I didn't bring much up, just the books, the batteries, a few different spices and the real find of the day, a tiny camping stove. No, that's far too glamorous a way to describe it. In one of Jessica's books it'd be a proper camping stove, one with gas cylinders and an oven attachment. And it'd be found next to a stash of freeze-dried food with enough fuel to last the rest of the apocalypse. Really it's nothing more than a small tripod upon which a saucepan can sit. Underneath there's a little tray for fuel pellets. It's basically the sort of thing you can build yourself with stuff lying around if you think of it, which, I'll admit, I didn't.

Now I can have tea, oh what joy! What true-blue Englishman wouldn't rejoice at such a prospect? There was no sign of any fuel pellets, though, so I'm making do with what I've got to hand, namely the wooden handles of my cutlery.

It takes an age, though. I stuck the small saucepan on before I started writing this entry and the water still hasn't boiled. Oh, how I'm looking forward to that first cup of tea!

All in all, things are slightly better than this morning. If I can come up with a way of using the flour, I think I've about fifty days' worth of food. Can you make cakes with just flour and water? I suppose I'll find out. It's far from a balanced diet, but it is calories.

How long does it take for scurvy to develop?

Day 6, 72 days to go

03:00, 18th March

I can't sleep. Of course I can't sleep. What the hell did I think, that a serene acceptance of my fate would manifest after I'd had a cup of tea?

What if no one comes? There. I've written it down. I didn't want to, out of some bloody stupid fear that writing it down would make it more real. The reality is that I've fifty days of food, which means sooner, not later, I'm going to have to go out into that living hell. I want to stomp and smash and swear and shout with the sheer unfairness of it all. But I can't. They might hear me. Have you ever tried to vent your frustration by writing down swear words? Try it, it's just not the same.

If I could walk properly, I'd be fine. I've not seen any of Them move faster than a brisk walk, not outside and not on the footage I saw online. I saw those shots from the traffic cameras in Rio; you won't have seen those, I bet. Hours upon hours of nearly identical footage as millions slouched slowly by. The military summary, and you won't have seen that either, reported their maximum speed at about five miles an hour and I can walk faster than that, any true Londoner can. Marching along, sidestepping traffic, tourists, and taxis while drinking a latte and making a phone call is practically in the citizenship test. But that's without a broken leg.

Even when the leg's healed, I'm not going to manage more than four miles an hour. Probably less. Definitely less. If the cast is due off in seventy-two days then I'll need a few months to build up the muscles again. At least for a few months, and how am I meant to survive that long? It just can't be done. When hunger forces me out, how am I meant to outpace the undead? I'll be slower than Them, and it's not like They're all going to be behind me. They'll be in front, to the sides, in the buildings above me, even in the sewers, for all I know.

If I'm being honest, and why the hell shouldn't I be honest? Being forced out of here by hunger in fifty days is the best-case scenario. Forty-nine days and three hours now, since I'll leave at first light. There are at least ten plumes of smoke in the sky. None are close enough to discern exactly where they are coming from, but that's hardly reassuring. If it turns into another dry year, then how long before the whole city catches fire?

Then there's the chance They spot me, and try to get in. It's easy enough for you to say, "Make sure They *don't* see you." What about hear me? What about smell me? They might as well have those senses as well as sight. Besides, if the zombies can't see *me* then neither can whomever Jen sends.

That is the problem, because, you see, I heard an engine. It definitely was an engine this time, and one that was quite close. It wasn't moving fast, just steadily, as if, and maybe it's just wishful thinking, but as if someone inside was travelling slowly enough to read the house numbers. Since I can't see much from my window, just the street immediately below and a lot of roof tops beyond, I hurried downstairs to get a view from the other side of the house. Except, of course, for me hurrying means moving agonisingly slowly.

I could hear the car getting closer, heading down the street, down *this* street, a slow rumbling interspersed with an odd muffled thumping. I was saved! Except it was getting closer and I was still hobbling down the stairs. I limped faster, giving no heed to the racket I was making, nor about any extra injury to my leg, not caring about anything except getting to the window and seeing that car. Jessica's room was closest. I hurried in, pulled back the curtain, and stood there, peering out into the gloom. I saw it, the most beautiful and terrible sight I've ever seen. I saw the red glowing lights slowly receding as the car drove away. It was an SUV of some kind and it was already a hundred yards down the street. It wasn't moving fast, barely faster than walking speed, but that's still faster than I can manage.

What to do? What could I do? I had to let them know I was here. I could be at the car in seconds. Minutes at most. I could go with them, I could escape, all I had to do was get outside and cross the few hundred yards that separated us. All I had to do… I tore my gaze from the car and looked down at the street below. There were dozens of zombies, more than I could easily count. The car was pulling Them along in its wake. The odd thumping sound was caused when it hit one of the undead. I'd not noticed, because I'd been looking for the car, but where there had been a handful of zombies a few days ago, now the street was packed.

Reflexive self-preservation kicked in, and I dropped to the floor. I actually dropped. That was impressive. At least, I'm impressed at the way my body reacted while my brain was busy being an idiot. The pain in my leg was immense. Needles of fire danced up my spine, and I bit my tongue to stop myself from screaming aloud.

I'd only been at the window for a few seconds, and I can only hope that the noise and the lights were such a distraction that the undead didn't see me. I retreated back upstairs as quietly as I could. I can't hear the car anymore. It's disappeared off to the west somewhere. So close. So far.

I don't think I was spotted, but I can't be sure. It's noisier outside now, that pervasive sound of shuffling has been joined by a banging clatter as They knock into cars, bins, and one another. I can't hear any sound from the doors downstairs, but I don't dare go and see. I don't even dare look out the window. If They know I'm here, then what? I'll be trapped, dead from starvation in under two months.

That was my rescue. I'm sure of it. Even if that car wasn't sent by Jen, even if it only came along my road by accident, that was my chance to be rescued.

06:00, 18ᵗʰ March

Oh, and it looks like They are just as active at night as in the day. So that's good.

16:00, 18ᵗʰ March

This morning, I fell asleep reading a book. It's called *Death Comes To Us All* by an E.R.K. Daley. I'm sure the title is a quote, but without the internet I couldn't tell you whose. Probably it's something Churchill said, either him or Shakespeare. Most quotes are. The book was written in the 1960s, and is about a post-apocalyptic, dystopian society surviving in a tower block, and as the story progresses, in underground farms beneath it. Each chapter advances the story five years, and at the end— well, no, I won't spoil it, you might want to read it someday.

It's an interesting enough book, an allegorical take on isolationism, but what's grabbed my attention are the ideas on farming. In the story, since the inhabitants are trapped inside with no access to land, and with their only resource being the light constantly streaming through their windows, they turn to hydroponics. They make a good go of it, too, but I think only because the author wanted generations who'd never been outside to grow old enough to rule.

What I'm wondering is how we're going to manage farming in the days to come. It's March now. Isn't that when crops should be planted? Who exactly is going to do the planting?

My focus was on getting people out of the cities. Evacuees like my tenants, at least the ones who made it to an enclave, would have found themselves crammed into a warehouse, church, community hall, pub, shop, or whatever other space was available and not absolutely essential to our immediate survival. They could look for a hotel room, or even a spare room in someone's house to stay in, but they wouldn't find one. By the time they reached Folkestone they would have found those taken by the evacuees from the nearby villages and towns deemed too difficult to re-supply or defend.

Housing Officers were appointed from the ample stock of now-redundant civil servants to ensure that every room was being used. Hotels, B&Bs, dining rooms, summer-houses, even garages, if it had a roof over it and plumbing within walking distance then someone could sleep there.

Families were to be kept together, and were to be billeted in the schools. This would allow some teaching to take place, but as the teachers were able-bodied adults more useful in other work, the lessons would be given by those too old to wield a shovel.

Sports centres would become hospitals staffed by evacuees, though they wouldn't have the resources to provide anything other than the most rudimentary level of care. The largest of the restaurants were to become kitchens for the masses, at least until the situation had stabilised.

Once everyone was within the enclaves, then the redistribution would begin. A mass forced migration of labour, both skilled and unskilled, some to the inland farms, some to the Irish Republic and the Scottish Islands, some to the Isles of Man or Wight. Others would be conscripted into either a fishing industry that I can only hope will provide enough for this first year, or the overseas reclamation operations, scouring the ruins of foreign civilisations for anything that can be salvaged.

There were some areas, such as between Lostwithiel and Wadebridge in Cornwall, where the rivers Fowey and Camel create a narrow stretch of land, across which defensive walls were to be built. The area inside this perimeter, once it had been secured, would be turned into a single massive intensive farm. Ancient hedges were going to be removed, the concrete ripped up and replaced with fields saturated with whatever pesticides and industrial fertilisers could be found. How the wall was to be built, and with what, I don't know, but the undertaking surely can't be beyond us, can it?

Inland farms, where supplies could come in and out by helicopter, were to be fenced in. Each was to have a nurse or doctor, a mechanic, and a member of the armed forces to coordinate defence. The locations were to be selected during that second week, between the announcement of the evacuation and the evacuation itself, but I have no idea whether the task was completed.

I thought only as far ahead as the next five months and gave no thought to the next five years. I assumed we wouldn't get a severe outbreak here. I thought that the rest of the world would be in such chaos there would be no competition for the overseas stockpiles. We'd be able to use those to get us through until harvest, and the immediate threat would recede after that. Perhaps it will, I have to hope it does, but just by looking out the window, I can tell we've had a major outbreak. How much rice and grain was stored in warehouses around the world, there for us to take? Did we even have the resources to collect it? What about the helicopters, the planes and the troops needed to secure the landing sites? As for fishing, where are the boats going to come from? We offered sanctuary to fishing boats that came in with their gear, but can there really be enough to supply sixty million people? Then again, looking out the window, it's clear we won't need to feed that many.

Maybe if I'd had a plan last night, I might have made it to the car, but would they have stopped? Would they have been able to tell I wasn't one of the living dead? I can't move quickly, and speed is about the only way of telling humans from the undead, particularly at night. The car would have ignored me at best, run me over at worst. Either way I would have been left for the horde to finish off.

Now, it's going to be much harder to leave. I can count at least fifty from my window. God knows how many are on the other side of the house, but I'll have to find out.

I made another assumption about our situation, one that's only just starting to dawn on me. I assumed that one day, one day soon, that these things outside, undead, zombies, infected, whatever, that one day They would die, and that we could just take back our island. What if we have to fight for it?

No matter. That isn't my concern, not now. Perhaps when I get out of here, but if I am to do that then I need to be fit. I started exercising this morning, I've done one hour so far, and will do another hour later. No, that's just procrastination and there's no place for that anymore. I'll do another hour now.

18:00, 18ᵗʰ March

I had to take a break halfway through, but that was about an hour's worth of exercise. It was close enough, anyway. Other than the occasional guilt-driven jog, I was an infrequent athlete. There's a certain type of professional politician who only wants to negotiate when you're both on a treadmill. It's an odd game of chicken; whoever quits first has to make the concession. It kept my waistline reasonably under control, but not much more besides.

But I do need to get fit. I'm still working out a regimen of push-ups, sit-ups, improvised weights, and stretches that work in a confined space and with a leg in a cast. If the world hadn't ended, I'd have published it as the next, must-have get-fit book. From the way my muscles ache rather than scream, so far I think I've done more good than harm.

I'll turn the phone off in a minute. I've had it on for half an hour. No messages, no signal. I've tried making a few calls, but can't get through to anyone. I'm pretty certain the network is down. There's no point wasting the battery. Might as well do some more exercise.

19:00, 18th March

There's not as many as there were this morning. They're still moving. I purposefully only did a rough headcount. I knew I wasn't in the right frame of mind to know exactly how bad my situation was. Presumably the undead followed the noise of the engine, and it's that momentum that's keeping Them moving hours after the last echo faded away. My neighbour, or what was left of her, finally disappeared sometime this morning. Now, the undead out there are all strangers. I'm glad of that.

Individually They don't seem to have any purpose, though They all seem to be heading in the same direction the car went. I've timed it, and They're currently meandering along at between one and two miles an hour. Those with visible injuries are a lot slower. My neighbour's probably not far up that road. I'm sure They were much faster this morning.

Are They just following one another, or do They somehow remember which direction the car went? That could be important, if I could only work out what the answer was.

20:00, 18th March

It's too dark to see now. That's almost comforting. I've moved my chair back so all I can see are the stars. When was the last time anyone saw those stars from this part of London? During the blackout in the Second World War, I suppose, but perhaps not. Even then there would have been searchlights criss-crossing the sky.

I've got the radio on, and I'm slowly twisting the dial up and down through the frequencies. All the BBC ones are still broadcasting the emergency message, but I sometimes think I hear something on one of the others. It's a distraction, at least, and a very welcome one.

The stars really are beautiful.

Day 7, 71 Days to go

05:00 19th March

I fell asleep in the chair. Not a good idea, as my neck can attest. Time for exercise.

10:00, 19th March

Pancakes! That's what you do with flour and water. Blimey, that took me long enough to realise. I've been staring at the flour for days dreaming of pizza, bread, and cakes, and then, for a change, I stared at the carton of powdered eggs and dreamt of fried egg sandwiches. But what do you get when you combine powdered eggs, powdered milk, and flour? Delicious, delectable, scrumptious, and a whole thesaurus of synonyms for... pancakes! At least, that's what you get if you add the magic ingredient, fire. That little stove is just absurd, totally unworthy of the name, so I caved in. I need to start taking risks, so I came downstairs and lit the fire.

I'm now on my fifth cup of tea, and sixth pancake. My plan was to make enough pancakes to last today and tomorrow, and boil enough water to wash, but I can't stop eating them. I know, I know, I should be rationing the food, but one day here or there isn't going to matter much.

The fire makes less smoke than I thought it would. That's good, but the coal's not lasting as long as I thought, which is bad. Okay, so I'm burning way more than I need to, but it's so great to be warm again, inside and out. It's the little things...

For the record, I would like to give thanks to the Ricardo Philippe Ramirez Institute for Oceanographic Research and Exploration, whose logos so gracefully adorn the packs of powdered eggs and milk. PRIORE had lobbied Jen last year to try to get an increased grant and a reduced tax bill if they transferred their operations to the UK from Argentina. Being a rather cash-strapped research group, they'd not had much to offer by the way of bribes, so gave her a crate of the rations they supplied their teams in the Arctic. They got the grant, but mostly because it was one up on

Buenos Aires.

Each crate contains a month's worth of supplies for a crew of eight, based on a diet of six thousand calories a day. If this had been one of Jessica's books, Jen would have left the whole crate. Sadly, all I got was a box of powdered milk and another of powdered eggs. So it goes.

Damn! The oil caught in the frying pan. That's the second time that's happened, but they're not my frying pans and there's at least three more in the house. Hey, I just realised. I could make an omelette without breaking any eggs!

15:00, 19th March

Nope. You can't. The best I managed was a sort of scrambled mess. Not that unpleasant with enough salt and pepper, but it's definitely not an omelette. There is, no, there *was* a place in Kensington that did the best omelettes. They were light and fluffy with just the right level of crispiness on the outside. They were so, *so* good. If we'd had a light week, I used to take the staff there for lunch on Fridays. I think they liked it, but perhaps more because I let them take the afternoon off afterwards and so, to them, being told it was omelettes for lunch became synonymous with a half day.

There were just the four of us, Charlotte, Sharmina, Ioin, and myself. Charlie and Minnie were both interns with ideas of standing for parliament. Ioin was an office manager with dreams of opening a surf-and-turf restaurant in Cornwall. The interns were a new thing. We were expanding as I moved away from consultancy towards more electioneering and policy work for... well, it doesn't matter now, does it? Jen was going to run for Mayor of London as a stepping-stone to the party leadership. We'd joke that it was our five-year plan. She stood a good chance, I think.

I got my three employees passes out of the capital. The last I heard, they were all going to Wales to stay with Ioin's family. That was two days after I got out of the hospital. Of course, it was difficult to stay in contact with the mobile networks down and with email being ropey at best, but I wish I knew if they'd made it.

18:00, 19th March

The emergency broadcast has all but stopped. It's continuing on the old Radio 4 long-wave frequency, but FM is now silent. Either there was a power failure at some substation or, with the evacuation supposedly complete and with no one left to hear it, the electricity was deliberately cut.

As for the broadcast on long wave, that's different to the one I've been listening to on FM these past few days.

"The time is eighteen hundred hours. This is an emergency broadcast. Stay inside. Avoid contact with the infected. If you are stranded in a city, indicate your presence with two or more white sheets hanging out of a top floor window. Listen for further announcements."

Brief and abrupt, there's no date, no names, no station call-signs, just that message repeated on the hour every hour. The only thing that changes is the time. But that mention of infected, that means it's not some old automated system. That message has been recorded recently.

19:05, 19th March

The message has changed again.

"Stay indoors. If someone with you is infected, kill them. There is no cure for the infection. Do not leave your homes. If you are able, hang a white sheet from windows on the first floor or higher. Listen for further instructions."

It's someone I've met, probably more than once. It isn't one of the usual BBC voices, but someone else. Perhaps someone from a university, or a junior ministry official, or is it just someone I met at a party? I'm really not sure. I keep listening, trying to place the voice. It's frustrating, almost makes me want to turn the radio off, but maybe they'll say something more, something useful.

I'm not sure about the white sheets. I'm worried that breaking a hole through the roof would just attract more of the undead.

Day 8, 70 days to go

05:00, 20ᵗʰ March

I've stopped taking the painkillers. There are only twenty-five left. It's not going to be enough if I take them one at a time, and one at a time doesn't do much good. Exercise is the answer. Got to get fit. Got to get out of here.

11:00, 20ᵗʰ March

Laundry time. I don't know why I put it off. The first batch is now hanging up, dripping tepid sudsy water all over the floor. It's wonderfully cathartic, except the smell of soap has now combined with that of the smoke to permeate the house. The change would be a relief, but even with the windows closed, there's a musty odour forcing its way in from outside. It's a bit like the smell you get in the countryside just after a torrential storm when the manure and decaying leaf matter has been churned up by the rain. Oddly, though, I prefer it to detergent.

18:00, 20ᵗʰ March

Cold, cold, cold, cold, cold. Far too cold for the laundry to dry. I've left it hanging up in Tom's flat, but what chance is there of it doing anything but rotting this side of June? Well, what's done is done. There's little lasting heat from the fire and I've burnt through most of the easily broken furniture. The flats downstairs are far too big and draughty to stay in. I'm starting to feel a bit guilty about the way I treated my tenants. Up here, under a mountain of sheets, and blankets it's just about bearable.

I've been scouring the AM band and have found a few foreign language stations still broadcasting. One is in French, the other is possibly Polish, though it could just as easily be Russian or Czech. There was something on FM earlier, somewhere around 99.8. It was faint, and indistinct, but I'm sure that the voices I heard were in English. Perhaps it was a pirate station somewhere. How far does an FM signal carry? Could there be someone in London with a generator?

I'm trying not to spend so much time watching Them. I start to panic every time I see one move, convinced it's going to head this way, unable to relax until it's disappeared up the road or returned again to that torpid crouch. It's not conducive, as Jen's grandfather used to say. But hiding here under the blankets, it seems… I don't know. I suppose I just want to be doing something.

18:30, 20th March

The radio is broadcasting a looped message. Yesterday there was a slight cough during the broadcast. It was there again tonight. Still, that makes sense. Why have someone actually in a studio twenty-four hours a day when they could be doing something productive?

Nonetheless, it's disappointing. That broadcast was my proof that there was someone else alive out there. I know that there's Jen and the evacuees, and I know that between me and wherever she is there probably are other survivors, but I can't be certain. This broadcast changed all that. It was proof, real tangible proof, that out there was a community with enough confidence in their own security that they risked searching for a broadcasting station, enough spare power to make the broadcast, and enough spare people to have one sit by a microphone. That cough has turned that proof into nothing more than evidence that someone *was* alive, once.

Seven o'clock and it's already getting dark. Exercise and bed.

Day 9, 69 days to go

10:00, 21st March

Woke up. Exercised. Washed. Ate the last of the cold pancakes. Then I went back to watching the undead. I know I said I wouldn't, that it wasn't healthy, but what else is there to do?

They've no economy of movement; rather, it's as if each command to each limb is sent separately and no new command can be sent until that individual movement is complete. Lift left leg, bend knee, let left leg fall, lift right leg, bend knee, let right leg fall. It repeats over and over until They hit an obstacle, then They'll edge to the left or the right and try again. There doesn't appear to be any conscious reasoning behind it.

They're still continuing their slow exodus. No, not an exodus. The evacuation was an exodus. Nor is this a migration. I need to stop describing Them in human terms, it's the sort of anthropomorphising that will lead me to think They're still alive. A flood, then? Or a torrent? A river flowing ever onward, never to join the sea?

No, no, no, that's way too poetical, especially for me.

All the zombies I'd spotted yesterday are gone, replaced by a new load. There's nothing much to distinguish one group from another. It's all the same mix of generic winter clothing. Wait. No. I've double-checked. I can't see any uniforms. Is that odd? I suppose that depends on where They are coming from. But with everyone who had one ordered to wear it, with the police and thousands of others hastily put into ill-fitting camouflage, then surely I should have seen some by now. Unless they decided to take their uniforms off. I suppose the soldiers who chose to stay with their families were deserters, after all. Oh, I know, you think that would be an obvious thing to do? Well, it would be, but it assumes the deserters would have had time to change clothes as well as have clothes to change in to.

Am I just reading too much into this? I used to do that all the time, extrapolating too much from too little data. It was why I was dreadful at predicting election results from exit polls.

I'm going back downstairs to make a more thorough inventory. Anything is better than sitting by this window. Other than a secret tunnel to a long forgotten but still well-stocked bunker, I'm not sure what I'm looking for, but if I'm going to leave here someday soon, then I'll need more than just the clothes on my back. Besides, going up and down the stairs very definitely counts as exercise.

17:00, 21st March

The basement! I'd forgotten about the basement! That almost warrants two exclamation marks. I didn't forget about it, not really. It's not a proper basement, let alone a cellar. It's nothing more than a long tunnel the length and width of the front hall, dug out to about five-foot-seven. I know that because I keep banging my head whenever I go down there. Like those in most Victorian houses this size, it was built as nothing more than a place to store the coal. There's actually a coalhole at one end, though it's now completely painted over. I suppose, in a pinch, I could use it as an escape route, but only if I could get outside and spend a couple of hours unsticking it. The basement contains the fuse box, the electricity meter, and whatever my tenants wanted to store down there.

I haven't been in the basement for two years, not since the fuses blew on Christmas Eve. I was meant to spend the holidays in Northumberland, but missed the last train to the north. This honestly wasn't my fault. What made it worse was that Jen and I had gone to the station together. We were both on the train when my phone rang. Since we were in a quiet carriage, I got off the train to take the call. The doors closed as I was standing on the platform and Jen laughed, she actually laughed, as the train pulled out of the station. Of course she did, she was going off to her parents' home for the holidays, while I was stuck in London until the garage where I stored my car opened again on Boxing Day. I arrived back here to find the fuses had blown and spent a very unpleasant hour rummaging through the accumulated detritus trying to find the box. Looking at the basement this afternoon, I'm not sure anyone's been down there since. But I digress. Victory and achievement and success! Of a sort...

No weapons, no hidden stashes of guns and food indicating that Grace was actually a Russian spy, and no secret tunnel. None that I could find anyway, but the basement is full of treasures. Most of it, in fact almost all of it, is useless in the current situation. There's some mouldering camping gear that could probably be resurrected, but I'm not planning to sleep outside. Similarly, if I was a bit more skilled, I could turn the weird electric thing that's either for curling hair or stripping paint into something truly deadly. As it is, I am resting on my laurels this evening over my find of a bike.

I'm not sure whose it was since I never saw any of them ride one. The wheels look okay, except that the tyres need pumping, but the pump was still attached. There's some rust on the frame, the brakes look more than a little dodgy, but all in all, it seems sound.

Yes, I know I can't ride it just yet, but the cast will come off. At worst I can always sling some bags on it and use it as a pack mule. I saw a lot of evacuees doing that.

20:00, 21ˢᵗ March

The bike got me thinking about transport and that got me wondering whether the car outside, the government one sent to collect me, is an automatic? If it is, then there's no reason I couldn't drive it. The keys, well, I know the driver turned the engine off. They'll be in the ignition or on the floor, or at worst, in his pockets. I guess the risk is in the time it would take to check whether the car would start. It's the risk of getting trapped inside the car with the living dead outside, pounding against the glass until it breaks. I did say I was going to start taking risks, but perhaps this is one too far.

Day 10, 68 days to go

09:30, 22ⁿᵈ March

Exercised then breakfast. One half-bowl of muesli, and that's the last of it gone. Another three days and I'll have finished my looted cereals, and then it's pancakes until the eggs run out. And then? No, I'm not going to think about that, not yet.

The car. I find my eyes drawn to it more and more. It presents an attractive idea of a quick escape, but how practical is it? Will it work? Where would I drive it? To the south, east, and west there's nothing but mile after mile of suburbs. Roads could easily be blocked by the undead. To the north lies the river.

My mind is as drawn to the river as my eyes are to the car. The Thames is only three and a half miles away and the undead can't swim. I'm only basing this on the video footage I've seen, but I'm pretty sure there weren't any reports about Them swimming. At least, not substantiated reports from reputable sources. There was hearsay and rumour of course, but there were rumours that They could fly and change shape, so I don't know if I should pay any credence to the ones saying They can swim.

Once I get to the river, all I'd have to do is find a boat and float out to the sea. That has to be easier than trying to walk, cycle, or even drive down to the south coast. With so much of the post-evacuation plan, what little of it there was, dependent upon fishing I'd certainly be picked up, wouldn't I? Even if the evacuation failed, especially if it failed, surely I'd be most likely to find other survivors at sea.

It's hard to think coherently. Is it because of the lack of vitamins or the lack of human voices? I've tried talking to myself, but I find it strange, slower than I can think and unsatisfying.

Focus. Stay Focused. The car. I've been looking at the car and replaying what happened, trying to work out if it's worth the risk.

The text came on 10ᵗʰ February at 09:12. I've still got it. It reads: 'Car coming. Maybe 1 hour. Be ready. Jen.' That was it. My last message from her. If my tenants had only stayed a few more days they could have driven out with me. Surely the four of them could have easily subdued the zombies out there. Even if the driver had still been killed, the five of us could have driven off. We could all have been safe.

When the message came I grabbed my jacket, threw my laptop and the hard drive into my bag and then sat by the window, waiting. By that time, I'd already seen a few of zombies. The first had been on the 8ᵗʰ, at around teatime. By then, the streets were deserted. I'd not seen anyone out there all day. I know it was teatime, because I was sitting by the window sipping a brew. My eyes were flicking between the street and the phone, waiting for Jen to call. That's when I saw him, just walking down the street. He was wearing a tracksuit and not a cheap one, but the kind professionals wear to run up and down mountains. At first I thought he was a solitary type who'd decided to wait until after the evacuation and leave when the streets were deserted. Perhaps he'd just bought the gear to look cool at the annual company away-day and finally he'd found a proper use for it. By the time he'd got level with my house I realised that it wasn't a he, not anymore.

There weren't any visible wounds, there was just something about the way that it walked that told me it was one of Them. It was almost out of sight when it suddenly stopped. I'm not sure why, but I think I heard a scream from somewhere not far off. It paused only a moment before heading in that direction, faster and more purposefully.

That was the first, and I saw a handful more before the car came, always moving, but never chasing anyone. Never attacking.

I was in the bathroom when the car finally arrived. It was late, almost two hours had gone by since I'd received the text. By the time I got over to the window, the engine was off, though the driver was still inside. Whether he was waiting for me, or whether he was checking the address, who knows? I was still debating if, since I didn't have his number, I should call Jen or should just open the window and shout down to him, when the car door opened. He got out. He looked up at the house and raised a hand to his eyes. I don't think he could see me through the tinted glass and was just shielding his eyes from the sun, but I waved back anyway. He took two steps away from the car, paused, then went back, bent over, and reached in for something, I think from the glove box. I couldn't make out what he was doing, but it took his full attention for half a minute.

It was long enough for a scrawny woman, she must have been at least seventy when she'd died, to claw at his leg. She had been in the alleyway that runs between the two houses opposite, hidden from his view and mine by the multi-coloured cluster of bins. Unlike every other one of Them I'd seen and every one that I've seen since, she wasn't wearing thick winter walking clothes; rather, she was dressed only in a thin nightgown.

I watched as he turned around. She raised a hand to his shoulder and pulled herself up his body. He grabbed at her arms and tried to push her

64

away, to hold her back, but she kept violently thrashing. Her mouth snapped open and closed. With each twitch and jerk, her teeth got closer to his skin. There was a pop as her right arm dislocated, and then her mouth could reach his neck. In two ferocious snapping bites, she'd virtually severed it. His body hasn't moved since.

But he did turn off the engine before he got out of the car.

11:00, 22nd March

Having difficulty planning lunch. I'm starting to feel hungrier more often. I thought if I spent more time planning the meals, it would help distract from the size of the portions, but I've not much variety of ingredients. It's going to be rice with herbs and spices. The only real decision is whether I should add oregano or thyme, paprika or cayenne.

They're moving faster. They're still slow, slower than I could walk. Slower than I *think* I could walk, but They are getting faster, as if there's something drawing Them in. Is it herd mentality or could there be some kind of hive-mind behind it?

No. There's no evidence of that. I need to stop thinking like that. It's just late-night horror show stuff. There aren't any hives or herds. I need to stick to what I know, what I actually know, that today They are moving faster than yesterday.

16:00, 22nd March

Outside of the UK and New Zealand I don't know of any country that turned off its mobile phone network. Even with the fractured internet, a lot of video footage was uploaded, particularly in that first week of the outbreak. Thanks to my government phone, I had access to it. I watched some of those recordings. All in all, I don't think my fellow Brits missed out on much. Most of it was phone-camera and webcam stuff that could be split into two categories: the forlorn goodbyes of those about to leave whatever safety they'd found, and the bloggers who saw it as their duty to chronicle the end of the world. I didn't see much point in either of those types, but there were a few genuinely interesting pieces that stand as a final testament to the macabre marvel of the Web.

My favourite has to be the pseudo-scientific pieces. I found them oddly reassuring despite their content. It was those videos that I was thinking of when I was trying to recall whether or not They can swim, though I'm not sure I ever saw a piece where they covered that. In some they dissected living zombies. In others they catalogued how to turn household objects into weapons, or categorically proved things like holy water, for instance, had no effect. Even I know it's from the wrong mythology, but it was clear, from the blogs, that others didn't. Then again, what has myth to do with this harsh reality?

There was footage from the space station where the last astronauts set the cameras to automatic before evacuating. There were the disastrous attempts made again and again by over-full ships trying to unload refugees on the Antarctic ice. And then there was the blog from the American Free Army.

The group, if you were to believe their own site, was based in Texas, but based on the exterior shots I'd say they were somewhere in Colorado. According to their hour-long vitriolic propaganda piece, they'd been preparing for the UN-Zionist backed invasion for decades, and this apocalypse was the result of us ignoring them. It was all our fault. They had declared themselves the natural successors to the United States government and they commanded all citizens… and so on. After a half hour or so of the worst kind of vitriolic paranoia, the cameraman took us on a tour of their bunker. I have to say that it was a good thing the zombies came, because there was no way the Feds would have ever dug them out of there. Their concrete bunker had three-foot-thick walls, underground tunnels, and a storeroom with enough food for a thousand people for twenty years. But the largest chamber was kept for the armoury. I think the quantity of their supplies is the reason they lied about their location.

The video finished with footage of them killing what they claimed were a handful of zombies in the woods outside, but to me they looked like refugees. That footage was uploaded on the 24th February, and I'd initially only watched it in the hope that there might be some practical advice. I stayed on their site because after that video finished, another started, and this one was a live stream.

I don't know whether they were just technically incompetent, or whether some hacker decided to embarrass them in front of the world, but the webcams they'd set up inside and out were broadcast over the Web. It was like reality TV when you really didn't care what happened to any of the contestants, and it was compelling, just as long as you kept the sound off.

There were about sixty of them in that bunker, split into four firing teams and a command and supply unit. Seriously, that's what they called it. Each day more zombies would appear, and each day they'd kill Them, yet more undead were always there to take their place, drawn in from miles around by the sound of gunfire.

Each day, the number of full boxes of ammunition in the armoury fell. On the third day, the leader told them to start making the shots count. "Aim for the head," he said. "One shot, one kill," he said, and he took to marching around the compound hitting the younger ones who were "wasting rounds." They tried, but they just weren't that good.

On the fourth day, at 16:04 GMT, someone went into the armoury and found it was empty. They were overrun thirty minutes later.

What got me about that video was that these guys in the bunker had no idea that the rest of the world was watching. You could tell from the conversations, from the bravado and banter that turned to bluster and threats, they thought they were talking in private. I don't know how many rounds they fired in the end, or how many zombies they actually killed, but not one of them knew anyone living outside who cared enough to call and let them know that the world was watching.

Day 11, 67 days to go

13:00, 23rd March

I need a plan. I need somewhere to head to and a way to get there. A goal, if you like, and one more purposeful than counting down the days until the cast should come off. Someone still may come for me, but with each passing day the chance of that recedes. If I am truly on my own, then I need to act while I still have the luxury of time.

If this had happened at any other time, or if our apocalypse had manifested itself in any other way, I'd have gone to Northumberland. Jen's parents' place isn't really a farm, it's more of a manor. There's farmland attached, but that's all looked after by tenants. At last count there was a dairy herd, six fields of potatoes, and an organic farm tied up in an exclusivity deal to supply courgettes to one of the London department stores. It's not exactly the makings of a balanced and varied diet, but it is food, and the farmers there know how to grow it.

Her parents are real-life aristocracy, the landed gentry, genuine minor nobility that can trace their stewardship back to the times they used to stand on the walls and square off against the Vikings. Not that there are any walls now. The crenelated castle burned down around the time of the Restoration, but the manor house that stands on the spot would be ideal to hold off the undead.

I suppose the question is whether the place would withstand a siege by the living as well. All over the world, there are, or were, millions of people looking for somewhere like that, somewhere that was obviously safe. If I managed to get there, would I find those people I knew still there? And that's *if* I could get there.

I'd have to use the government car. I can't see any other way of travelling that far. If the car still works, of course. If the battery's not dead, and if there's enough petrol in the tank. If I can get up enough speed to push through and out of London. If the roads north aren't blocked and if, when I get there, there's someone there who will take me in. Too many ifs. I know the bridges over the river were closed during the crisis, but did they remove the roadblocks when they evacuated? Probably not. Looking out there now, the street is so packed with the undead I don't think I could drive through Them. No, I know I couldn't. So the car's out, and without it there's no way I can limp to Northumberland.

Provisionally, the new government was going to be based on the Isle of Wight. Eventually any journey there would be by sea. One option is to head south to either Portsmouth or Southampton, where a large coastal enclave was going to be created around the two ports and the New Forest. How far is that? I wish I had a map. About eighty miles, I think, but that's as the carrion-crow flies. How far would I have to travel? That's a very different question and one that's impossible to answer. But let's say I'm lucky, and miraculously, somehow, don't have to take any detours, how long would it take? If I was healthy and fit, four days. Since I wasn't close to fit before the outbreak I'd say, without the cast, five. With the cast, ten days? Twenty? I really have no idea. That's without detours or hiding out for days on end, or the time it would take scavenging for food. What chance is there, what real chance, that I would actually make it on foot?

There's another way. The river. I've no idea how to sail a boat, but would I have to? If I could get on board one, couldn't I just ride it out to the coast? Surely I'd get picked up by a fishing trawler or some naval vessel, or maybe I'd be spotted by a satellite, for there's no reason why they shouldn't still be working. Certainly, I'd have a greater chance out on the water than I would here. There are, or were, dozens of houseboats dotting the banks of the Thames. I don't know how many of them have engines, let alone fuel, but all I'm really looking for is something that can float.

Or I could stay here and scavenge from the surrounding houses. Except, if my tenants are anything to go by, the rationing will have left the cupboards pretty bare. Soon what's left will start to spoil, and then what? How long will it be before the government tries to take back the city? What will I do if a fire starts nearby and I'm forced to leave?

No, staying here isn't an option. It's three and a half miles to the river. That is by far the shortest route, so it's now the official one. But not today. Not tomorrow either, there's just far too many of Them outside.

Day 12, 66 days to go

04:30, 24th March

I was woken in the middle of the night by the sound of scurrying. It was just after eleven and like a child terrified of the monsters in the dark, I hid under the duvet. It might have been a few minutes, it might have been half an hour before I slowly, quietly, sat up and reached for my crutches. The noise stopped. I waited, trying to get my brain to fire on at least half a cylinder. It wasn't a zombie, that was clear enough. There was some light from the stars, but not enough to see by. I fumbled for the torch, but caught myself in time. There was no way I was going to risk Them seeing a light through the window.

Just as I was starting to calm down, just as my heart's pounding was slowing to the point I could count the beats, I heard it again. I jumped with shock. I actually jumped. The sound stopped. This scene repeated twice more before I'd woken sufficiently to realise it was a mouse.

This is the first time I've ever heard one in this house. It's in here somewhere, and it likes to prowl around my room at night. I'll try to find it as soon as it's light, and while I'm at it, will box up all the food.

I couldn't get back to sleep. I tried, but I was too excited because, you see, if mice can survive then why not cows or sheep or pigs? One day, and it may be long off, but one day there will be bacon again. It might be mouse bacon, but that will do for me.

17:10, 24th March

The long-wave broadcast has changed. It's a different message, a new one. They're back to broadcasting music now, Bach, I think, or Beethoven. It's something funereal. The gist of the message: The government has fallen, we're on our own.

18:10, 24th March

This is what they said:

"This is Radio Free England, transmitting from the emergency broadcast station at Lenham Hill. We followed the emergency broadcast thinking we would find some remnant of the government here but the station was deserted. The message being broadcast was pre-recorded. We have taken over the station and have this message for anyone who can hear us. The government has fallen. All governments have fallen. The evacuation of Britain failed. The infection had spread too far and to too many." There was a pause.

"That is the bad news. There is good news, of a sort. This is a secure location. We have helicopters. We are prepared to use these to evacuate those currently trapped in cities and towns. We are also prepared to re-supply those of you able to hold your current positions. The only way that we can win back our planet is if we fight." Another pause.

"If you can hold out where you are, then you must. Please pay attention to the following instructions. If you need evacuation then display two white sheets from the roof. If you need re-supply, display two coloured sheets. If you do not have sheets, use paint. If you do not have paint, improvise." There was a slight chuckle. "I bet you're getting good at that if you've survived thus far. If you have supplies to spare for others to continue the fight, display four sheets of the colour of your choosing. We will broadcast further instructions and whatever news we can over the coming days. Good luck."

18:30, 24th March

I'm not quite sure what to make of it.

19:15, 24th March

I think it's Mahler. I'm not sure. I was never into classical music, but it's a different track, that's the important point. The music is changing. Someone is there, reading the message, changing the music. But what's happened to Jen? And where is Lenham Hill? It's a vaguely familiar name, but I can't place it. And how do you follow a radio signal? Presumably using the same skills that allow you to transmit on an emergency broadcast system, but is it something I can do? No. Of course not. But I can follow a map. If I had one. Tomorrow I'll look for one downstairs. If I can find

Lenham Hill, and if it's near the coast, then perhaps I can sail a boat there.

I've got sheets, more than enough. How do I get them onto the roof, though? And how would they ever see them? Are they using satellites? And would they be able to rescue me from here? Is it worth the risk?

I suppose the bigger question is whether I want re-supply or rescue.

21:20, 24th March

Do they really have a helicopter? Probably. Are they actually going to help? Or are they really just after the places that have supplies?

Day 13, 65 days to go

08:00, 25h March

The water pressure dropped overnight. It's now coming out of the tap at a thin trickle. I've refilled the bath and am filling every container I can find. Then, soon, I'll have to light the fire to boil it. I don't know how long standing water remains potable, but it can't be more than a few days.

15:15, 25th March

I've filled every container I can. I'll do it again tomorrow. Taken some sheets from downstairs. Too tired to try to break a hole in the roof now, maybe later.

The radio is just playing music now. An announcer comes on every so often to repeat that message, but there are no further details. I wish they'd say what the music is, though. It's annoying me that I don't know. Who are they? The only maps I could find were tourists' ones of central London. Where is Lenham Hill?

Day 14, 64 days to go

14:00, 26ᵗʰ March

I'm exhausted. My arms ache, my left leg is sore, my right isn't any better, and my back feels like it's going to explode. The simple act of filling a container with water, then moving it a few yards over and over... I must have about three hundred litres now, including the bath downstairs, the toilet cisterns, and the hot water tank. Maybe more. Do I mean pints or litres? I'll count again.

It comes to one hundred and twenty litres in the bath, two hundred in the hot water tank, eight litres in each of the toilet cisterns. Add to that the kettles, and pots and jugs, and I'm going to run out of things to burn before I run out of water to boil.

Day 15, 63 days to go

10:40, 27ᵗʰ March

The pressure dropped again. The zombies are still shuffling by outside, still moving, but with less direction. Would I be able to get through Them? Probably not. There are twenty out there now. I'll wait a few more days, see if They disperse a bit more. It's not really the undead outside the house I'm worried about; it's the others between here and the river.

I can't just go straight north, I mean I can try, but I can't see it working out that way. Even with diversions it'll only be five or six miles. That's about two hours, normally. With the leg, call it three hours. Add on another couple of hours to find a boat, though how hard can that be? I'll just look along the river until I spot one. It's all less than a day's journey.

The radio people have changed their message:

"This is Radio Free England, please listen carefully. There are more survivors than we thought. We will be able to reach all of you, but not immediately. We have a virtually unlimited amount of fuel, but a limited number of pilots and limited room here. If you can support other survivors in your current location please display four sheets on the roof to let us know. Only together can we triumph."

There was more, but that's the gist of it.

The roof itself is directly above my ceiling. It wouldn't be too difficult to break a hole through the roof, but that would knock off dozens of tiles. The undead would certainly hear that. But let's say I did it, that I hung up a sheet, wouldn't the noise of a helicopter overhead just summon more zombies from all around? And then, since there's nowhere to land, wouldn't I just be left trapped without any chance of escape?

I'm going to try to make a small hole, but only a small one, and only to see if I can.

17:30, 27th March

It's a lot harder than I thought. My ladder is locked up in the storage bin outside, so I climbed up onto the desk. That wasn't easy, but I can just about reach the ceiling with the tip of the knife. I could probably make a hole, but not without knocking the tiles down to the ground, and even then, it would take days.

That's not really why I'm reluctant to follow the instructions on the radio. It was the tone of the broadcast. There's something about it that I don't like. I can't work out what, though. Is it my natural distrust of pretty much everyone, or is it something more?

Day 16, 62 days until the cast can come off

18:00, 28th March

Today was spent packing and repacking a small bag that I found downstairs. Dry socks, underwear, some canvas shoes for when the cast does come off, the last couple of chocolate bars, two packs of sunflower seeds, the small stove, and two litres of water. That's as much as I can carry. After an hour of standing in the hall wearing the pack as practice, I was exhausted, and it's nowhere near enough.

I need to assume at least three days on a boat. That's three days of supplies, and I just can't carry that. I'm still unsure about the bike. With a crutch in each hand, will I be able to pull it as well? I can picture myself holding onto the handlebars and hopping along, using the momentum to move further and faster. Picturing it and actually doing it are two very different things. Nonetheless, it's the only way I'll have enough to survive. I've filled three bags with extra food and water bottles. One on the handlebars, one hanging on the frame, the third at the back. I'll make it work.

Day 17, 61 days until the cast comes off

09:00, 29th March

Thirteen zombies outside. That's the fewest I've seen so far.

I've added a knife to each of the bags. They're carving knives from the rather nice set Tom had, and are the only alternative to the hammer that I can find. Stab or crush, that's what my world has devolved to, and it took only a little longer than a month.

Day 18, 60 days until the cast comes off

13:00, 30th March

Now there are fifteen outside.

If only I could ride the bike, I could cycle out of here. If only I could walk, if only I could run, if only I could just sprint through Them… but I can't. If it wasn't for this leg, if I'd not slipped on that staircase, then I'd be in some bunker somewhere eating military rations, not constantly worrying every time one of those things turns its head towards the house.

I don't think I'll ever escape

Day 19

A few more zombies, a few less. What does it matter?

Day 20

A lot more. Too many to count, going by in a slow and steady stream. There must be hundreds, and thousands more that I can't see. I can't move faster than Them. I can't sail a boat. I don't even know how to start the engine of one. I can't use my arms to fight unless I drop my crutches, and that would make me a stationary target. I don't have a map. I'm running out of food. I don't have any proper weapons. I can't carry more than a couple of days' worth of supplies.

Even if I get to the river, and let it carry me out to sea, then what? The ocean is a massive place. Really, and I mean really, what are the chances I'll be rescued?

The water pressure's dropped again.

Day 21

There's no chance to leave. Not now. There are hundreds of Them outside. I daren't even light the fire, just in case They see the flames through the curtains. I should have sealed up those windows properly. Where are They going? Why are They going there?

I'm stuck here, then. Leaving would be suicide.

Day 22

The horde keeps coming. How many are there? Thousands? Tens of thousands? Is the same scene being played out across all the streets of London? Hour upon hour, day after day, the noise isn't loud, just persistent and pervasive, an unceasing thudding and hissing and scraping and rattling and cracking, as this never-ending army of golems marches on. Oblivious to the shattered glass on the street, heedless of obstacles, ignorant of fatigue, it just keeps coming. Will it ever stop?

Day 23

I'm down to twenty little blue pills, now. Would that be enough, if I took them all at once?

Day 24

11:13

The water's stopped.

14:00

Nothing I can do about it. Nothing. The water's stopped. The plug in the bath didn't fit properly, and I didn't realise. That water was my margin, the only thing keeping me alive. If I can't go outside, if I have no water... I needed that water.

You can last for three weeks without food, maybe longer. But water? Three days. Three days without water and I'll be dead.

18:00

I've come to sit on the stairs. For me this counts as a holiday. There are no windows, so there's no chance the undead can see me, and just as important, no way I can see Them. I've just over fifty litres of water. Not as much as I'd planned for, not nearly as much. It was stupidity. It was laziness.

I'd emptied the bath. I should have filled both of them, but I didn't. I thought one would be enough. One bath for water storage, the other for washing clothes. One bath for drinking water should have been enough.

I turned on the tap, letting it fill from the hot water tank. In turn, the tank would refill from the mains. Except the plug in the bath didn't fit properly. As quickly as it was filling the bath, the water was trickling down the plughole. All I managed to do was drain the water tank. I kept sticking my head into the bathroom, checking whether the bath was full, but my attention was on breaking up wood for the fire. I didn't notice until I went into the kitchen to get a drink. When nothing came out of the tap, I first went to check the taps in the kitchen next door. By the time I thought to check my supply in the bath, all the water had drained.

I'm left with about fifty litres, call it forty-five after I've boiled it. If I don't wash, then I can get by on about a litre a day, but since I've only about twenty days' worth of food, I don't suppose it really matters that much. As soon as I can, I have to leave.

19:30

I'm savouring a cup of tea, carefully tasting every last drop, trying to preserve the memory of it. It's going to be a long time before anyone brings any more of it to this island.

That got me thinking about the things I'll miss the most. Things like steak, conversation, hot showers, those will come back. Not any time soon, sure, but they will come back. Other things, like books, movies, and new clothes, they'll take longer and when they return they'll be different. Books will be shorter or perhaps only printed online. Perhaps there will be no new films, just recordings of plays, broadcast in theatres during the harvest when the actors are too busy reaping crops to learn their lines. Clothes will be duller, more functional, and maybe all made of wool, but they will come back. But tea? How long before a community in India or China has enough food it can start growing tea again? How long after that before it can export it to the other side of the world? The same with coffee and chocolate. Maybe there are plants somewhere in the UK, maybe at Kew or maybe some hobbyist was growing some in their greenhouse, but what are the odds those plants survived?

Tea, coffee, chocolate, there's probably enough boxed and sitting in warehouses around the world to keep the survivors stocked until the stuff spoils, but how soon will that be? Ten years? Five? For chocolate it must be less, maybe a year. One year until there's no more chocolate. Not in my lifetime, anyway. And where exactly are these warehouses?

Steak. I could really go for a steak about now, but how many cattle will survive? The evacuation plan assumed there was enough breeding stock on the islands to restock after the immediate crisis was over, but if the evacuation failed what are the chances any cattle survived? I've seen footage of zombies attacking livestock, but I've also seen footage where They left the animals alone. There seemed to be no pattern to it, and the only theory I have is that the undead will attack anything that's between Them and their real prey. It's a weak theory, and I'm not sure how relevant it is because I don't think the cattle will be able to survive without humans, and no humans who survived would be able to resist eating any cattle they found.

Fusion power will never happen now. Nuclear power will become a thing of the past. Air travel, too. If we're lucky, we're going back to the age of steam.

On the bright side, no more laundry for a while.

Day 25

10:00, 6ᵗʰ April

I could probably collect rainwater through a hole in the roof, but how many calories would I use up creating it? Too many, I think. I've got the bike downstairs ready to go. The day-pack is next to it. I'll keep the day's ration of boiled water on me at all times. I'm ready to go the moment there is a let-up outside.

The signal strength of Radio Free England has weakened. It could be the radio, but I think it's the signal. The message is the same; sheets on the roof, wait for help. There are no signs of helicopters over London and I'm sure I'd hear one. You used to be able to hear them all the time, even when you couldn't see them. I don't think I'll be getting any help from Radio Free England, even if I did trust their message.

Day 26

05:00, 7ᵗʰ April

I spotted it around eleven last night. I couldn't sleep, I was just sitting in my chair, staring at the rooftops when I saw a light go on in the top room of the house opposite.

I wasn't sure I'd seen it at first, it could have been a reflection, it could have been my imagination, but then I saw it again. Still, I wasn't sure it was anything more than a fire. To be frank, that was what caught my attention. My secret dread is being forced to choose between burning alive inside or being eaten alive outside.

Then the light went out and a few minutes later, three, I think, it came back on. It was hypnotic, mesmerising, and I just stared at it. What I didn't think to do was to mark where it was coming from. There are fifty-seven windows visible from here, any one of which could hold the light's source.

I'm getting ahead of myself. I have no possible way of knowing whether someone was actually signalling. Even after all this time it could be a phone flashing that its battery was finally running out. It could be some kind of alarm or, well, anything battery powered. And that doesn't mean a person, at least not an uninfected one. Maybe there was someone in there, once alive, now undead, reflexively flicking at a button. Maybe, but probably not. The light flashed six times that I saw, the last time being at about half twelve, but I stayed up all night watching and thinking.

10:00, 7th April

I've lit the fire downstairs. A pillar of smoke by day might just be the ticket. As there's no point wasting the wood, I'm boiling up some water, and having a celebratory cooked meal, too. But I couldn't leave the fire burning and come up here to watch the windows. That's too great a risk. So I've got to hope that whoever is out there saw the smoke and realised that the fire might just come from a room on the other side of this house.

I'm going to need a better way of signalling.

14:00, 7th April

I haven't seen many horror films, haven't seen many films at all recently, but there's one scene I remember from a zombie movie where there's a guy in a gun shop who has no food, trying to talk to people in a mall who have no guns. They're a few hundred yards away and communicate with a whiteboard and binoculars. I've no whiteboard, no binoculars either, but I do have paper and Blu-Tack.

It took me a while to think of something useful to say, "Hello" being too short, "Are you alive" begging for the response of "No," and "Hello, is there anybody out there?" being, well, unoriginal.

In the end, and wanting to put something up, I wrote "R U There?" spread onto three pieces of paper and stuck to the top of the window in Tom's flat, since the tinted glass in mine is almost certainly going to make it illegible. There are seven windows that I can see from my room which I can't see from his. I just have to hope that the other survivor isn't in one of those.

There are, I suppose better things I could have written, and not much I can do if the response is "Yes."

Time for more smoke signals.

16:00, 7th April

Nothing yet. It might be that this person is only awake at night, shining the light out in one direction for a few hours then going to a different window, and repeating it. Or they've no paper. It'll be dark in a few hours, I'll signal back.

17:00, 7^h April

I didn't notice it earlier, simply because my mind was on other things, but there's only a handful of Them out there today. They don't look as formidable as the others. Some are missing hands or arms or, in one case, most of a leg. If I'm going to leave, it would be a good idea to do it sooner, not later.

It would be too late to leave tonight anyway. I'll think about it tomorrow. But whether there is a reply or not, I *will* have to think about it tomorrow.

20:00, 7th April

Flashing the torch on off, on off, on off, pause. On off, on off, on for a minute, off for five minutes. Adding Morse code to the list of skills I wish I'd bothered to learn. So far, no response. No response from the undead either.

23:00, 7th April

Nothing yet.

Day 27

02:50, 8th April

Still nothing. The batteries are running low. Time to call it a night. I'm returning back upstairs.

06:40, 8th April

Up early. Maybe the light wasn't visible from downstairs. I don't want to risk opening the balcony doors, though. Did I imagine it?

09:00, 8th April

There are two of Them out the front, two out the back, with another lurking around a side street about a hundred metres west. I think that last one is stuck there, maybe immobile, maybe sleeping. If They sleep. Whichever it is, the creature's not moving. Of the others, the two out the back are sort of heading southward, slowly pinballing across the street from one side to the other. One of the creatures at the front is heading roughly southeast, I think. It's hard to say since it's moving in a curving zigzag. The other one isn't moving at all.

All of that is a long-winded way of saying that if I'm planning on leaving I should do it soon. And I should definitely head north. It's fifty-two days until the cast is due to come off, but, with the help of the crutches, I can stand for three or four hours at a time now. Going up and down the stairs is getting easier, and I can't delay much longer. Getting to the river is my only option.

I think if I'd heard a single helicopter overhead I might have stayed, I might have knocked a hole through the roof, hung out white sheets, tried to get more food from nearby houses, whatever. But I haven't. Wherever Radio Free England is, they're staying clear of south London.

I'm ready to go. I should go. It's just... What if there's a reply tonight? What if the reply comes five minutes after I've left?

10:15, 8ᵗʰ April

A reply! It's written on paper on the window of a house about seventy metres away. Too far away to be legible.

12:00, 8ᵗʰ April

I've no binoculars. Think. Think. Think.

13:00, 8ᵗʰ April

If the writing's too small, increase the font size. One word spread out on two sheets, spelling "Escape?"

13:30, 8ᵗʰ April

He, or she, has got it. The message has been replaced with three sheets of paper, a letter on each one, spelling "Y.E.S."

17:00, 8ᵗʰ April

We've found a way to communicate. It's about as basic as it can be, each word spelled out one letter at a time, each letter held up for a minute.

I don't like that, writing 'he or she,' it's too impersonal I'll call him/her Sam. My neighbour's name is Sam.

Our conversation so far:

Me: "Escape?"

Sam: "Yes". Then a blank sheet. "No Water"

Me: "Water. Food. 20 days. You Come Here?"

Sam: "Then 10 Days Water." Pause. "Then What?"

Me: "Escape Now. Where? River?"

Sam: "Can't Swim. Ha. Ha. North."

Me: "How? Car? Petrol??"

Sam: "Bike."

And there it was. Oh well.

Me: "Broken leg. Bike = hard."

Then there was a long pause. Seven minutes without a response, the longest seven minutes of my life.

Sam: "Car. You Alone."
Me: "Yes. You?"
Sam: "Yes."
Me: "Escape Tomorrow?"
Sam: "3 Days."
Me: "You Water. 3 Days?"
Sam: "Yes. Plan Later. Food Now."

And that's it, thirty-six letters, numerals, and assorted punctuation stuck to the windows over a couple of hours, and we're going to escape in three days' time. That's as far as we've managed to get so far. Now there are the details to sort out, like where to get a car from and where we'll go, but at least now I won't be alone.

20:00, 8ᵗʰ April

Our conversation continued. We're leaving at nine in the morning three days from now. Day 30, by my count.

I asked "Which Car?" Sam replied "Mine", which is reassuring. Sam probably has a car parked out front. I'm pretty sure those houses all had their front gardens converted to drives. Obviously Sam didn't want to drive before because a bike is less likely to break down and can probably get further in a day if the roads are blocked. Which, I'm guessing, they probably will be. That's why I've been against trying to drive out of here. The last thing I want is to get stuck on some narrow country lane somewhere. But, if Sam wants to drive, then I'm not going to worry. If there is a problem then we'll find a solution. Two heads and all that.

If his car's out front, then would it be better if I went over to his house? Or is it safer if he goes out the front and drives around? It's difficult to know. I'll sleep on it and see what he thinks tomorrow.

Day 28

13:00, 9ᵗʰ April

Two days to go!

Not much conversation today. The strange thing is that we don't really have much to say to one another, at least nothing that can't wait. I'm guessing that Sam, with the exception of having two working legs, is in pretty much the same situation as me, working out what will be essential for the next part of the trip.

Where in the north we're heading I don't know. For now it's enough that we're going to get away.

16:00, 9ᵗʰ April

I'm packed, ready to go. I'd like to leave now, but I can see the wisdom in staying put as long as possible. There's still the chance of rescue or of the undead finally dying, and there's no point wasting food, but… It's just that there are fewer out there than ever before. They could be back in greater numbers at any time. But we have a plan. We'll stick to the plan.

Should I take the laptop and the hard drive? All those files Sholto sent, are they of any use to anyone now? They take up so much room I wasn't going to take them when I was planning on leaving on foot, but if we're taking a car, then why not?

Day 29

06:00, 10ᵗʰ April

Breakfast, then as soon as Sam's awake we'll really need to finalise our plans.

10:00, 10ᵗʰ April

I'd just stuck a message up, when I saw Sam walking out of his house. He glanced up briefly at the window, long enough for me to make out his scraggly beard. He didn't wave. I thought for a moment something had happened, maybe the undead had broken in and he'd been forced to leave. I thought he might be heading here, needing rescue. Before I could even turn to go downstairs and open the door, he'd turned his back, and begun to head up the road.

One of the undead spotted him and started to follow. He glanced over his shoulder, occasionally checking its progress, but he didn't stop, he just sped up, easily outpacing the zombie.

He's getting his car, I suppose. Either that or he's leading Them away, making our escape easier. Wish he'd told me, though, because if he's bringing a car back today, it'll draw hundreds of Them with it, like the SUV did. I need to be ready. Bag by the front door. Ready to run, or limp as fast as I can, just as soon as I hear him coming.

12:00, 10ᵗʰ April

No sign of Sam. I'm in Tom's room, watching the road. It'll be easier to get to the front door from here.

18:00, 10ᵗʰ April

Where is he? I suppose he's gone for the car, and he'll bring it here tomorrow morning. That makes sense. Maybe the car's in an underground garage somewhere. Can't think where one of those could be around here, though.

21:00, 10ᵗʰ April

No sign of him, which is good. He's sticking with the plan. His car was probably in a garage somewhere. Maybe he works there. No, more likely he knew someone who had a car and spare petrol stashed somewhere in south London. He'd have seen the SUV and how it drew Them here, just like I did. That's why he's waiting until tomorrow. He's sticking to the plan. The question is whether I stay up here and watch for him or whether I go downstairs and wait by the door.

22:00, 10ᵗʰ April

I just timed it. I can get downstairs from here in two minutes, and I could have done it faster if I wasn't worried about noise. I'll stay up here and watch, in case he can't get the car through the streets and parks it somewhere. That's a real possibility, I suppose. I mean, with all those fires I've seen, houses could have collapsed. Maybe some of the roads are now impassable. I'll just wait until I hear a car approaching, then it's straight downstairs and out the door. Not long now.

Day 30

15:00, 11ᵗʰ April

Seven minutes. After I told him my leg was broken, that's how long it took for him to decide to leave me behind. Not just leave me behind, but to guarantee that I wasn't going to come with him. Why else give a time and day for our escape?

Seven minutes.

I can understand why. The broken leg made me a liability and maybe if I'd come up with more of a plan, something to make the risk worth taking, then it'd have been different. But I didn't. Even so, it took him only seven minutes to decide to leave me behind.

I don't think I would have done that. If it had been him with the broken leg and me with both legs working, I don't think I would have walked away like that. No. I know I wouldn't have left him. Maybe if I had a child or someone else already injured to protect, I might have, but if it was just me, on my own, I'd have helped. I would have at least tried. I would have, at the very least, spent longer than seven minutes thinking about it.

18:00, 11ᵗʰ April

I'm not going to forgive him. I'm never going to forgive him, and when I get out of this I'm certainly going to find out who he is and, well, we'll see. I can sort of understand why he did it, but I'll never forgive him for it.

I would have stayed and helped.

Day 31

09:00, 12th April

Slept in. Why not? It's quiet outside. My morning routine was severely disrupted by the lack of zombies to count. One out the back, only barely in sight.

12:00, 12th April

This morning I walked up and down the stairs for two hours with the pack on. My muscles ache but it's a good, healthy ache. I kept it up almost non-stop, and managed it without making too much noise, at least by my reckoning.

I wish I had a bit more space to practice with the crutches, but I think I'll be okay. Thanks to my absent tenants there is no issue with laundry, and clean clothes help somewhat since I'm not able to wash.

I've an amusing image of my tenants huddling together in some hideout, having escaped who knows what. They're hungry, thirsty, dirty, and decide to come back here, where they know there's a bit of food and at least some clean clothes. Only to find, when they break down the doors, no food and their clothes are all stained.

But they won't be coming back, will they? Maybe I'm just projecting my anger, but they, too, left me here without even a note to say they'd gone. They knew my leg was broken. They knew I was stuck here. They may have assumed that I'd be fine, thanks to the visits by Jen and her uniforms, but they could have left a note. Common decency should have demanded it.

I've about eighteen days of food and water left.

14:00, 12ᵗʰ April

I might have been a bit optimistic on the food front. Some of it is already a bit... well, I'd throw it in the bin if I dared go outside. I think I've got about nine or ten days' worth of food that I can't take with me. That's settled it. That is when I leave, nine days from now.

I've no map beyond the tourists' ones of central London. Since I'm not planning on seeing the sights, I'm going to head towards London Bridge. There was a restaurant there, just by the river, where I'd meet lobbyists that Jen couldn't be seen anywhere near. Nice place, good coffee, horrid food. It was perfect for when you wanted a meeting to last just long enough to find out how much and what for. Once, when a meeting was cancelled, I took a walk along the river and found a cluster of houseboats. I stared at them for the best part of an hour. They seemed so out of place among the old warehouses long-since converted to flats. I even daydreamed of buying one, one day, when I could afford to move out of here. Anyway, that's where I'm heading.

I'll have to unmoor the boat. I mean, they didn't look like they were undocked and driven up and down the river at weekends; they looked permanent, but they can't have been held on by more than rope, can they? Probably they can. I've no way of cutting through a chain, acetylene torches not being strictly required in the landlording business.

If I remember correctly, access to those houseboats was through a locked gate in an iron fence that ran the length of the bank. The fence was at least six feet high, with curved spikes at the top. The gate's got to be the easiest way in, so I'll need a way to break the lock. Of all the tools I can find, I think the chisel is my best bet. And if it's not strong enough? Then I'll just have to double back to where the concrete balustrade is, climb up and over, and then swim out to the boats. It's about thirty feet, I think. Can I swim that far? I'm willing to try, but then what?

In Jessica's books there's always someone in the group who knows how to drive or fly whatever vehicle they find. Brad, who hasn't said or done anything yet in the story, happens to be a trucker. Helicopter? No problem, Stacy was an hour away from getting her flying licence. Stealth

90

Bomber? De nada, Captain Hernandez here is actually an NSA operative based at Area-51.

No such luck with me. If I can't work out how to turn the motor on, or if they don't have a motor, then all I've got to do is to fend the boat off the bridges as I let the current carry me out to sea. That can't be too hard, can it? I'll just need an oar or a plank of wood. I think I can manage that.

So now I have a goal. The bigger challenge is how to get there. You see, I don't really know this area. I worked on the other side of the river. I lived at the office. Slept there, too, as often as not. Around here, I know where to buy milk, where to catch the bus, which road leads to the park, but as for which road offers the quickest route to the river, your guess is as good as mine.

16:00, 12th April

The bike looks ready to go. I've got a selection of tools, spare clothes, the radio, and rope in bags slung on either side of the rear wheel, with space for the last of the food and water. I've strapped a broom handle between the front and rear wheels so they won't go their separate ways. When I get to the boat I'll tie the broom handle onto the end of the crutch and can use that to push away from any bridges or floating detritus. I really think this can work.

The laptop and hard drive go into my backpack. It's a lot of weight, but I promised Sholto, and I think, especially after Sam, that promises should be kept.

17:00, 12th April

I thought I heard a helicopter. I'm not sure. There was certainly something, it sounded unnatural but in a good way, a mechanical and completely artificial way. I went to the window to see if I could spot it, but I couldn't even tell which direction it was coming from. I didn't look too long, or too hard, as my attention was immediately caught by the sight of a vapour trail.

That truly was a sight to behold, though it affects my plans not one iota. There are still people out there, enough of them to maintain and fly jet planes, and with some purpose that brings them over London.

18:00, 12ᵗʰ April

Those beautiful white scars have been obscured by clouds. The plane might have been coming from overseas, heading to one of our airports. Before the evacuation, it was weeks since there had been anything except military flights coming into the country, but the runways were all kept clear.

Overseas it was a different story. There, it seemed as if half the people who were escaping headed to the airports. Cars were driven onto runways, planes were overloaded, and the infection was carried onto the few flights that managed to take off. We retasked the satellites, and sent jets to fly over and check, but other than a few military bases there isn't a safe landing strip south of Tromso or north of Addis Ababa. Or there wasn't when the evacuation started. That's over a month ago. Who knows what state the UK's airports are in, but if I was a pilot and I managed to get a plane in the air, this is the only place I'd know I might stand a chance of landing it.

I didn't see the plane, just the vapour trail. Maybe it's a private jet, maybe a passenger plane, maybe a fighter. The type doesn't really matter, just that someone out there flew it.

Day 32, eight days until I leave

11:00, 13ᵗʰ April

Radio Free England stopped for a few hours this morning. A broken substation, a failed transmitter, or maybe they just decided to stop, I don't know the cause. They gave no explanation when they came back on air.

Clothes ready, pack's packed. I'm ready to go, but I just don't want to. This place, it's not much, but it's mine. I've survived here for thirty-two days. Longer, really. I've been on my own since I came back from the hospital. That's fifty days. Fifty-three since New York. That's a long time to survive in this new world.

If only I could stay in here longer, but I know that I can't.

12:00, 13th April

Would that government car have anything inside worth taking? Perhaps the driver even had a gun. I'm sure he was carrying one in the hospital.

I'll check the car as I go out. I'll lean the bike up against the rear door, check the driver for keys, and a weapon. Yes, he'd have a firearm, wouldn't he? They were issuing those to everyone, police included. It didn't matter if you were in admin or on the front line, if you wore a uniform then you carried a gun. I'll check the boot first, and if there's time, the glove box. Or should I check the glove box first? Wouldn't he keep a gun close to hand? If he didn't, if it was in a locked box in the car, then I'd never find it. I just wouldn't have time.

Do I see if the car starts? No, I've already decided against that. Who knows what the roads are like? A bike's far more sensible.

Day 33, seven days until I leave

06:00, 14th April

The car is looking very tempting. The more I stare at it, the more I wonder what's inside. Maybe there's a walkie-talkie or a radio or something.

07:00, 14th April

Of course there's a radio, whoever it is that Jen detailed to pick me up is going to have a way of communicating with the rest of the squad or platoon or whatever. Perhaps even with Jen herself. If I'd taken the chance when the car arrived, I could have been rescued long ago!

A working radio, and emergency supplies. I'd be able to stay here until someone came. But what if they didn't come? What if the Radio Free

England people were correct, and there's no longer any government? No. I don't believe that. I've no reason to trust those people. I mean, what about the Royal Navy? It's not as if the undead could sink a submarine. But what if, wherever they are now, the range is too great for the radio? What if they don't answer? What then?

Well, then I'd have the extra supplies from the car, wouldn't I? There's got to be enough for at least another month. Enough until it's safe to take off the cast and I could leave here actually pedalling a bike rather than just pulling it along. I'd be far faster than any zombie. It would be safer. Much safer.

17:00, 14th April

I went downstairs. I was going to go outside, see if I could get to the car, but there's one in the back garden. It's sort of squatting there, right in front of the door. I couldn't see it from the window; it's hidden by the angle of the house. I'll need to kill it.

Sam probably noticed it. That's why he didn't come any closer. He'd seen it and it'd seen him. It wasn't Sam's fault. He'd committed to helping me, but after he'd been spotted he had to escape. It wasn't like he had any choice. Now I feel bad for him. Maybe we'll meet up when this is over, perhaps on some ship out in the Channel, and we'll talk and laugh, and he'll apologise, and it'll all be cool.

I don't know if the creature was drawn there by the noise I've been making over the past weeks, but it was within two paces of the door, so close that if I'd been unaware of it, I'd surely have walked right into it. It's old, well over sixty, male, and wearing a suit and tie. Sort of dressed in its Sunday best. I wonder if he always dressed like that, or if he'd dressed up for the evacuation. No, that doesn't make sense, who wears a tie to go on a hike? So, not an evacuee. Who was he?

It's impossible to tell the quality of the suit. The sleeves are tattered, it's torn at the knee, and covered in blood, dirt, and stains I don't want to identify. There's a story, a long terrible story, behind the man and how his life brought him here to my door, a story that will have to end tomorrow morning because I need to get that radio.

94

Day 34, six days until I leave

06:15, 15th April

I'm going outside now, to get the radio, grab whatever else I can and then I'll come back inside. But I'm going to be cautious. I'm going to be clever. The undead can't be clever, you see, that's where I can beat Them. This house has two doors, see, that's the clever bit, I'll go out the front, and try to get to the car without any of Them noticing.

Maybe They are so far gone by now, They won't be able to smell or hear me or whatever They do. I'll go slow, but if I am spotted I'll lead Them away from the house, then I'll sneak back in from the other side.

I'm going to take the bike with me. This will be good practice in case my plans change and I have to use it in my escape. See, I'm planning now, planning ahead.

06:30, 15th April

Damn. There's one out the front, it's not moving fast, but it is moving. Killing two of Them is not part of the plan. I'll just wait.

11:00, 15th April

Damn, Damn, Damn. It's just sniffing around the door. Did it hear me? It must have done.

12:00, 15th April

It's gone. Not sure where. Can't see it from any of the windows. Too late now. Going to wait until tomorrow.

16:00, 15th April

One of the last videos I watched before the power went out was of a group in a compound in Colombia. My Spanish isn't very good and I couldn't tell if they were FARC, a drug gang, or just some group of like-minded citizens whom fate had trapped together. There were thirty-six men and women, all well-armed, with the oldest being about sixty, the youngest not yet old enough to shave.

The footage, which had been uploaded live, started with each one saying a few words to the camera. These weren't goodbyes; I understood enough to tell that. They were exhortations to the people of the world, a call to rise up and make a stand. As each person said their piece, you could see the others behind them, nodding, psyching themselves up. By the time it got to the last one, the youngest, the crowd was chanting along, waving those oh-so-recognisable AK-47s in the air.

They were in a courtyard of some kind, with big thick wooden doors, double the height of a person. By the time the kid finished, two of them were standing by the doors. Everyone else stood in two lines facing the doorway. A man who hadn't spoken before stepped forward. He was dressed as a priest, though like the others he carried a gun. He gave a short speech, as much to the camera as to his comrades, his flock. I couldn't work out much of what he was saying, not until the last few words. "Though there is a lot to fear, what we should fear most is fear itself. Walk with God and we shall restore this Garden of Eden." Then he blessed them all and took up a place at the front.

He counted down, "Tres," and the others joined in, "Dos. Uno." The doors were thrown open, and they fired. Slowly they advanced, one step, two, the ones at the front firing until they'd emptied a magazine, then one in the rank behind would step forward and take their place.

They advanced as far as the door before the first of them was killed. A zombie that'd been shot, but not in the head, rose up and tore at the legs of a woman in the front rank, pulling her to the ground. Her screams were cut short by that kid, now in the second rank, who fired a single shot into his comrade's head before shooting the zombie and stepping into the gap.

The boy died less than a minute later. When the priest saw the child fall, something in him must have snapped. He fired until his gun was empty then he rushed forward swinging it like a club. That's when the camera was dropped. It still recorded and uploaded the footage, but from its position on the floor all that could be made out were the bodies dropping one by one as the sound of gunfire slowly faded.

96

That is the fear of going outside, the fear of an uncertain death, set against the almost certain death that awaits me if I stay here and risk nothing. But I will go. I have to go if I want to live, and above all, I do want to live.

Day 35

05:30, 16th April
This is it.

Part 2:
An Empty England

16th April - 13th June

Day 35, The Walworth Road, London

19:15

Killing the zombie in the garden wasn't as hard as I'd been dreading. I opened the door and swung myself forward two paces. Letting the crutch dangle from the loop I'd attached to my arm, I took a firmer hold of the hammer I'd been awkwardly gripping with my right hand. As the zombie started to rise, I adjusted my stance. Better balanced, I swung down just as the creature turned towards me, the blow landing just above its right ear.

The noise is something I won't forget, a cracking, sucking sound as the skull shattered. I won't forget the sight of that brown, sludge-like ooze spraying out, either. I don't know what a brain should look like, but I'm sure it's not that. The zombie collapsed onto the path, and that was that. It was over in a matter of seconds. Everything was going to plan. I pulled the bike outside, closed the door, and began making my way down the path.

The bike didn't work, not like I'd hoped. Perhaps if I'd been able to practice… but I'm glad I brought it because there was another zombie, invisible from the house, hidden behind the low front wall. I didn't notice the creature until it lunged at me. Its legs were gone, along with half of its jaw. It couldn't move far. It couldn't move fast, but if the bike hadn't been between us, I'd now be one of Them.

Reflexively, I let go of the bike. As the creature tried to claw at me, its arms became tangled in the frame. I froze. I just stood, staring at it for I don't know how long. I tried to lift my arm, but it was like moving through water. All I could hear was my own silent scream. All I could see were its crazed eyes flecked with grey, vacant but still very human. I brought my arm down, but there was barely any force to the blow. The hammer glanced off the side of its head, bringing away a chunk of hair, flesh, and brown pus, exposing the white skull beneath. I struck again, and again, and again. It stopped moving after the fifth blow.

I was in shock, I suppose. I left the bike there. I didn't even try to disentangle it. Time didn't slow down. I wish it had. If anything, it sped up as *I* slowed down. Every step seemed to take an age as I limped over to the car. I told myself to focus, to stay on task. I'd get the radio and then get back inside, call for help, and a helicopter with an extraction team would arrive before nightfall. Foolish!

It seemed like an hour had elapsed before I reached the far side of the car, but it can't have been more than a minute. That's when I saw the driver properly. His head, lolling forward, was held on by a few inches of grey sinew. His unseeing eyes stared at nothing. As I nudged his body with the crutch, trying to move it aside to see if the keys were underneath, his mouth gaped open. I jumped, and nearly fell over as I stumbled sideways. From the safety of my home, through the illusory security of my window, the idea of moving him, searching him for his keys and radio, it all seemed so simple, but this…

He was dead. Properly dead, I mean. It took me a long while to realise that. I guess I'd known it at some level since, in all this time, he'd never moved. Why didn't he turn? Perhaps it was because he'd been almost decapitated. Or maybe it's something else, something to do with the way he died. I don't know.

I began searching. There was nothing on the ground, which meant I had to check the body. His insides were already putrefying, held in by nothing more than his clothes. There was a radio, tucked onto his belt near his back. That went into my pocket, and that was zipped closed. After all I'd been through, I didn't want to lose it.

That's when I should have gone back inside. I'd found what I wanted, but success had made me complacent. I kept searching. His pockets contained nothing except a lighter, a pack of cigarettes, and a couple of ID swipe cards. No gun, no holster, no keys. I scanned the ground again, and spotted the keys near the rear tyre. They must have been kicked there when he was attacked.

I hobbled over and picked them up. Since I was there, I took two steps round to the back of the car and unlocked the boot. It was empty. At least it looked empty. Maybe the emergency supplies were in a hidden compartment. It's more likely that, wherever he brought the car from, they were so low on supplies that the emergency gear had been removed. The back seat was empty. That left the glove box. I decided to go around to the passenger side rather than try to move the corpse out of the way. I was nearly there, my hand almost at the handle, when I saw two things: the silenced pistol lying in the driver-side footwell, and the third zombie, the one who'd stopped me leaving yesterday.

I stared at it. It glared back with those unblinking grey-flecked eyes, and shuffled closer. Its mouth opened and it let out... not a moan, not like in the movies. It was more a hissing, guttural grunt of escaping air as its lungs were compressed while it moved. It was a far more inhuman sound than anything I was expecting. What made it worse was that it was coming from a firefighter. She was wearing the protective jacket, the thick boots, and trousers. I doubt she'd donned them to tackle a blaze, but those thick clothes must have appeared bite-proof.

Perhaps I should have killed it. Hindsight's a wonderful thing, but I think I could have, and made it back inside afterwards. I might even have had time to check the glove box and properly search the boot, perhaps even time to remove the driver's body and see if the engine worked. Perhaps.

It was twenty feet away and getting closer, and I was still gripped by fear-laden indecision. The gun was only four feet away, but on the wrong side of the car. There was no way I could reach it without getting into the car on the passenger side and twisting forward. I don't know if it was loaded. Running around my head were scenes from movies where someone tries to fire, but the gun just clicks because the safety catch is still on. The only guns I've fired have been shotguns on pheasant shoots. I've no idea what a safety catch even looks like.

What I needed was enough distance between me and it that I could retrieve the gun, and kill the zombie without risking my life if I couldn't get the weapon to work. What I needed was not to panic, to stick to the plan. Instead, I turned and fled.

I limped as fast as I could to the end of the street, turning left because I was on that side of the road. I ducked down the cycle path running along the back of the next block. I didn't even think to check it was clear. It *was* empty, but by the time I got to the end, and back onto a main road, two of the undead were on my heels. I went down side roads and alleys, doubling back on myself, trying to head towards my house. I told myself to get a grip, to calm down and think, but all I could do was keep looking behind. Two became three, became four, then five and I ducked down another alley, across a cul-de-sac and straight through a laurel bush, tripped on a low brick wall, and hit my head as I fell.

I crawled under the bush, curled up as close to the wall as I could manage, and lay quietly, barely breathing. I couldn't outrun Them. I couldn't fight all of Them. I just hoped that They wouldn't hear me. I think I passed out for a time, maybe for an hour, maybe for two.

When I came back to myself, I held my breath, closed my eyes, and listened. There was plenty to hear. It was a veritable symphony of trees blowing in the light breeze, the drip of a broken pipe, the scurrying of something too small to concern me. Then there was the noise of the undead. It was at least a few streets away, a clattering snuffling sound as They slouched along, knocking into each other and whatever lay in the roadway.

Slowly, painfully, I got up. My leg had been knocked about during the chase, and when I stood, it didn't waste a second letting the rest of my body know it. Going by the chunk I'd torn out of the cast, I must have fallen over the wall a lot harder than I first realised.

As I left the garden, it took me a moment to realise I was roughly a mile south of my house, on a street that ran parallel to the railway. The alleyways were used as a pedestrian cut-through to the station, one that local residents had wanted to get closed due to the late-night traffic. It was completely the opposite direction to the one I'd wanted to go.

Since heading north was out, at least for the moment, I headed southeast, trying to put distance between myself and the undead. I moved slowly, each step far more painful than it had been at the beginning of the day. My breathing was more laboured, and I knew I wouldn't be able to keep going for long.

I killed my third zombie a half hour later. I'd found a cycle path that follows an almost straight line between Crystal Palace and Greenwich. It cuts through parks, across supermarket car parks, and along railway cuttings. While it offered a quick route to the river, it's a narrow path. In most spots it's enclosed either by the high walls of the buildings running alongside or by the fence that was meant, in some unfathomable way, to make it safer at night. It was that fence that kept me on the roads as much as possible. There was a greater chance of meeting one of Them, but also more options for getting away.

The zombie was in the middle of a footpath, about thirty feet from the road. It was facing towards me, looking straight at me as I walked around the edge of a high brick wall. If I'd been more cautious, if I'd gone a different way…

It came towards me at a fast, stilted walk. I didn't panic. I don't think I had any panic left in me. I looked around for an escape, but it was moving faster than I could manage, and then it was only a few steps away.

I flailed at this walking corpse with the left crutch, trying to push it away. That meant putting more weight on my right leg, which screamed in agony. The zombie raised its arms and batted at the crutch. Its momentum pivoted it around so it was sideways on to me. I shifted my weight onto my left leg, let the crutch fall to dangle from its strap. I tightened my grip on the hammer, and swung with all my strength.

The first blow knocked the zombie down, but my own impetus carried me forward another step. My weight was now completely on my broken leg. I stumbled, almost collapsing on top of the creature. My right leg stuck out behind, I shifted my weight to my left knee. The inhuman monster snarled, snapping at me with its broken-toothed mouth. The blow must have done some damage, as it moved jerkily. Its arms groped out, clearly unsure where the threat was. I brought down the hammer a second time. It died.

I picked myself up as best I could, and limped away. The leg… I'm worried I've done something serious to it, but what can I do? I needed to take one of my painkillers but couldn't afford to have my senses dulled. I tried to focus on something else, anything else, and that's when I realised that, when I spotted the creature in the alley, it wasn't in that half crouch the undead adopt when there isn't any prey. It was upright, waiting.

What had I done to give myself away? If it was smell, They would have known I was in the house or under those bushes. Perhaps the living dead can still see, but not as well as humans. After all They didn't notice the light when I was signalling to Sam. In this case, since I couldn't see the zombie, there is no way it could have seen me. That left sound. Instead of listening for Them, I started listening to myself. My breathing was loud and laboured. I began to take shallower, slower breaths. Then I heard the sound of my crutches. It wasn't that loud, but it was a rhythmic clip-clunk. I paused by a brick wall, tore off strips from my shirt, and wrapped them around the crutch's rubber feet. It was an improvement. I took my time at corners, and cut through back gardens so as to avoid the streets They were on, doubling and tripling back so many times that I am thoroughly exhausted.

I found a laundrette, maybe a mile and a half from the river. There's nothing at all useful here except intact windows and a door that was easily broken with the chisel and just as easily secured again by pushing a washing machine in front of the doorway.

Looking back on the day I think I saw less than twenty of the undead. I was expecting more, a lot more. I'd imagined a dash to the river with thousands chasing me. Then again, I'd imagined staying a few paces ahead, reaching that community of houseboats, and slamming the gate closed just before They reached it. As far as I thought about killing any of Them, I didn't think of it as anything more than swinging my arm. They would fall, and I would move on. I didn't think of it as killing at all, not really.

And the undead can hear. I've suspected it, but today I had proof. It's obvious, really, every time I emptied the sink or bath, or flushed the toilet, They heard water running through the waste pipe to the drain by the side of the house. Sam must have been doing the same, and with the same sorts of sounds coming from different ends of the street, They couldn't work out exactly where the noise was coming from. As their numbers began to thin at about the same time the water ran out, the conclusion seems sound.

As theories go, this is both a helpful and a gloomy one. It suggests there aren't that many zombies in London. If that's the case, why hasn't the government sent in the military to deal with Them? Does this mean the government really is gone? That's a question I can't answer today. It's one of many, like why didn't Jen's bodyguard turn into one of the undead? Had he used the vaccine? I suppose that's the most obvious answer.

Oh, and the radio? It was broken.

Day 36, The Walworth Road, London

05:30

There's a huge plume of smoke hanging in the sky to the north. It's bigger than any I've seen so far. The buildings are too close together to properly gauge how far away it is, but wherever it is, it's large enough to block out a whole section of sky. I'm not generally one for omens, but this doesn't bode well. I just have to hope it's north of the river. I can't smell burning, though. I'd have thought I'd have been able to, but that musty, noisome tang is so strong here that I can't smell anything else.

I'm just finishing breakfast, a tin of pineapple chunks. That's my last tin, leaving not very much left at all. Ah well, at least the bag is lighter. This isn't a bad place. There's nothing here, but the walls are solid, the windows are unbroken. I suppose laundrettes and drycleaners had nothing worth looting.

12:00, Bermondsey, London

Lunchtime. And joy oh joy, a change of pace. I'm no longer hungry. I'm actually satiated. Stuffed. Fed. Gorged. I've had sufficient unto the day thereof. Well, okay, that's the slightest of exaggerations. I'm no longer hungry, and isn't that the greatest feeling of them all?

I owe my full stomach to my distracted brain. No matter how hard I tried to concentrate, scenes of the evacuation, the official ones that they broadcast, went through my mind this morning. I'm not quite sure what triggered it, perhaps a survival reflex to avoid thinking about the horrors around me. Whatever, I don't care. I'm trying to avoid introspection.

Before the main evacuation started, during that period when everyone was at home and the government wanted to keep it that way, the press tried to emphasise why people without a permit shouldn't attempt to travel. There was this one piece, an interview that Jen gave at Paddington Station. She was explaining to the camera how important a gradual evacuation was in order to not overload the system. In the background, surrounded by smiling but armed soldiers, were quiet, orderly queues. They were made up mostly, but not exclusively, of boarding school children interspersed with the hostage families of those workers being kept in the city. Not that the reporter gave any explanation of who the evacuees were. As for Jen, all she said was that "those of you clogging up the roads, and trying to get on the trains, are just slowing down the evacuation of people like this." While pointing meaningfully at a group of very young kids. Then there was a choreographed Q&A session that lasted about five minutes.

Behind Jen was a vending machine. Every thirty seconds or so, someone would leave the queue, go over to the machine, and put some money in. The machine was empty, long empty, I guess, so the evacuee would head back to the unmoving line. A few seconds later, someone else would leave the queue and try the machine. It was weird. I counted it happening eight times during that short piece. All these people, they could see the other evacuees try. They could see them walk away empty-handed, but it was as if not only did they distrust the other people, they distrusted the evidence of their own eyes as well.

By the time I'd been released from hospital, most of the looting had stopped. There were occasional raids on supermarkets and supply depots, and those were put down very publicly. I saw some of the combat footage, all taken with helmet cameras and relayed to a 'Forward Combat Command Centre', where the video was scrutinised to identify whether any of the 'hostiles' had been undead. The looters were shot down without mercy or hesitation, no prisoners were taken, no warnings were given, none were left wounded. I think that in the videos I saw – and I must have seen at least twenty – in none of them were the looters armed, and in none did any appear to be infected. They were just hungry.

The following morning, the news bulletins would start with a reporter in a barricaded car park. The bodies had been taken away, but the ground was littered with damp patches where a half-hearted attempt had been made to clean away the blood. The reporter would then say that a number of looters had been stopped and the Food Distribution Centre would open shortly. The camera would then slowly pan across the car park, lingering on the bullet holes that riddled the stained concrete. And that was it. No further details were given and against that backdrop, none were needed.

As the reporter finished, in the corner of the shot, you could see hundreds of people queuing to get in for their day's meagre ration. Usually they were careful not to show the queues, not the real ones anyway. When they were doing a segment on rationing, they always used the same out of the way, immaculately clean shop with its equally immaculate customers. People would line up outside, chatting quietly, waiting patiently for their turn. None seemed bothered by the soldiers. Perhaps those customers were military themselves, dressed in civvies and glad for the easy duty.

The rationing system was pretty ad-hoc. For those in boarding schools, living on university campuses, in retirement or nursing homes, stranded in hotels, and so on, an individual was designated to collect the ration on their behalf. For the rest it was one ration per household per day. The size of the ration was determined by the size of the household, and that was calculated by counting the family members physically present in the queue.

Rations could only be collected from a specified distribution point, and only between the hours of nine and five. The only proof of address that was accepted was a TV licence. If you didn't have one, tough. If you couldn't find it, tough. If you turned up late, or couldn't persuade your teenager to get out of bed, tough. If you didn't want to risk any of your family having to walk the increasingly dangerous streets, well then, you would get a one-person ration and the rest of your family would go hungry. And if you were even suspected of bringing along people who didn't live with you in an attempt to get more than your share, then you'd be lucky not to be detained. It was a very poor system, everyone knew it, but it only had to tide the populace over for a few weeks until the evacuation proper.

The little shops weren't subject to the centralisation of supplies, the closures, and the rationing. It just wasn't practical to send troops to empty their shelves, not when you consider how many of them there were and how little stock they carried. It was even less after people realised they were open when the supermarkets were closed.

I saw three today, all looted, their windows broken, the shelves inside torn down. Weeks of wind and rain had finished the work that the hungry masses started. But small shops aren't the only places where there would be food. After remembering the image of Jen at Paddington Station, I went looking for vending machines. It turns out that they are everywhere. It was simply a matter of finding somewhere that had been closed from the first day of the curfew.

The obvious places will have been picked clean long ago. Train stations, shops, and restaurants aren't worth investigating. Somewhere I'm sure would be worth checking would be the warehouses where they stored and prepared all the airline food, but I'm nowhere near an airport. Hospitals stayed open too long. Schools and universities might be worth a shot, but not all schools had vending machines.

Gyms, at least this one, are a veritable treasure trove of energy bars, protein shakes, glucose drinks, and whey powder. I'm not sure what whey powder is. Something to do with cheese, I think. There's dozens of tubs here, all claiming to be protein-rich and banana flavoured. I miss bananas. Sadly, no real ones were harmed in the making of this stuff.

They seem to be clumping together now, which is a mixed blessing. On the plus side, it means there are stretches of road where there's not a single zombie in sight. On the negative, if one spots me, five or six others will be on my heels before I can blink. That's meant I've headed more east than north, and I've still not seen the river, but I'm close! Outside there's a sign pointing the direction of a footpath that goes along the South Bank. There's no distance given, but it means the river can't be much further.

This gym's a decent-enough place. There's more food and water than I can carry, a back door, strong front doors, and no broken windows. I could probably hide out here for a week or two. But, now I've got this far, I'm going on. I could be at the river this afternoon, and floating down the Thames by nightfall. The bag's filled to bursting with sports drinks and energy snacks. By the time I write the next entry, I'll be on the waves!

19:00, Bermondsey, London

It's all gone to hell.

After I closed the gym doors behind me I secured them with a bit of cord. It wasn't a great knot, but it *did* need to be cut or untied, a feat I'm sure is beyond the undead. I stuck a note to the door that read 'If the cord is still tied, this place should be zombie-free'. I thought someone else might need somewhere safe to hide up. As it turns out, that someone was me.

After an hour, I'd travelled half a mile northeast. The plume of smoke I'd noticed earlier is somewhere to the northwest. I've been trying to angle away from it. I don't know whether this is grim schadenfreude, but that plume, I think, is over Whitehall.

I saw a few zombies. Not many. Maybe one or two per street, but enough were positioned at crossroads and corners to force me through narrow alleyways and the narrower gaps between buildings. If I don't have to face Them, then I'd rather not. Call it cowardice if you like. I prefer to think of it as prudence. All the time, as I was sneaking along, getting closer, metre-by-metre, I kept thinking how few of Them there were.

A couple of years ago, I found myself with a few days to spare in February. On a whim, I decided to get in the car and go and stay at the coast. I've always liked the seafront in winter. There was something about the sight of the waves crashing against the beach, of rain pouring down windowpanes when you're safely inside that appealed to me. So I got in the car and headed south. I'd been hoping to find a quaint B&B, but ended up in one of those dreary chain hotels. The first thing the next morning, I got in the car and drove back.

109

When I got home, everything looked the same but something felt wrong. The door was still locked and nothing was missing. It was only when I went to make a coffee that I found the water in the kettle was still warm. It turned out to have been Jen, I'd not told her I was going away and she'd dropped by looking for some feedback on a speech she had to give to the National Union of Teachers. All was well, and we laughed about it afterwards. Walking through London this morning, I got that same sense of unidentifiable dread, as if the other shoe was about to drop. Something, I didn't know what, but something was wrong.

The buildings I passed were looted, ransacked, or otherwise without promise. They were certainly not worth the time to investigate when I could almost touch the river. Above me the Shard cast its long shadow over the streets below, where a few cars had been pushed onto the pavement to keep the roads clear. Then I came to the barricades.

A bus had been wedged diagonally across a road. Behind it were a couple of supermarket delivery vans and an upended skip. Around and behind those was a great mess of wood and rubble. At first, I thought this was the result of some bizarre accident, so I continued on to the next street. That too was blocked, this time by a more professional agglomeration of concrete, barbed wire, and sheet metal.

It was the same on the next road and the one after that. Every street that led to the river was blocked, and in front of the barricades were the undead. They clustered in front of the barriers in greater numbers than I'd seen before, pawing at them, as if They were trying to get to what was on the other side.

When I realised that, my heart skipped a beat. Could there be survivors there? Could those who'd stayed behind to keep the city working during the evacuation be just a few feet away? I listened for any trace of life, but all I could hear was the whispering grind of metal on metal. That's when I started to worry. I knew there had been roadblocks on all the bridges, but those had consisted of nothing more than traffic cones and easily moved waist-high fencing, not this towering amalgam of steel and cement.

From what I'd seen it must extend across a good portion of the riverbank. It was too big an enterprise for it to be done by some small group since the evacuation. It had to have been planned and organised. That meant the government and that meant Jen, and she'd not told me about it.

I was only a few hundred yards south of London Bridge, a distance of about three miles from my house, and it had taken me two days to travel it. I wasn't going to turn back. I wanted to see the river. More than that, I *had* to see it.

I thought about climbing the barricades, but the undead had congregated at each likely spot. I thought I could face two of the undead, possibly even three, but often there were eight or nine or even more.

Carefully and slowly, I inched my way along the roads parallel to the Thames. What I needed was a building that fronted onto the river, one that I could access from this side of the barricade and walk through. Failing that, I needed a building tall enough that, from its roof, I could at least see how far the barriers extended. Either way, I needed to find it fast. I was beginning to tire. I was a few hundred metres south and east of Butlers Wharf when I saw three of the undead in the street in front of me. Three was too many. I ducked into the doorway of an accountant's, levered the lock apart, stepped inside, and closed the door quietly behind me.

There was a staircase leading from the reception area, so I headed up. The first floor was split into three conference rooms, all ready for use save for a thin layer of dust. It looked like no one had been there since before the outbreak. There was a second set of stairs, less well kept than the first, carpeted only as far as the landing, at which point they bent out of sight from the hallway. I went up again, driven by a desire to get high enough to see the river. At the top was an open plan area with cluttered desks. I ignored those and headed for the door marked 'Access Only'. It was unlocked and led to a flat roof dotted with dead plants and faded plastic chairs.

Finally, I saw the river, a hypnotic sliver of blue-green. I can't recall whether there were any boats on it because, after that fraction of a glimpse, my eyes were drawn away and down to the streets on the other side of the barricades. There, I saw the undead.

There were thousands. Tens of thousands. Maybe millions, maybe the entire population of the country north of the river. There were more than I could count, and all that was between Them and me was the haphazard barricade of concrete and steel.

That wasn't the worst of it. You know the old nursery rhyme, 'London Bridge is falling down'? They'd demolished the bridges, or tried to, but there was a narrow section of pavement still standing. It was perhaps three feet across with the balustrade intact on one side, and on the other, an overturned Army truck. Around that narrow gap the living dead were tumbling into the river, but through it hundreds were being funnelled across the bridge onto the already densely packed streets of the South Bank.

The sound I'd heard was the shuffling of thousands of feet pushing forward, of bones breaking as the zombies at the front were crushed, and the groaning of metal as the barricades strained to hold.

I can't be sure whether the undead spotted me as I stood there, or when I turned to flee, or even if They spotted me at all, but as I raced to the door, the noise grew to a deafening moaning roar. Underlying it was a grating screech as the barriers began to move.

I practically fell down the stairs and ran outside, heedless of noise, of my leg, of anything, but I'd forgotten the three creatures I'd entered the building to avoid. They were waiting right outside the door. I swung the hammer at the closest, but missed; my aim was spoiled by the weight of the crutch. I hobbled forward, futilely shoving at Them with the crutches. Then I gave up and limped away as fast as I could. They followed.

I ignored the pain in my leg. I didn't even have the breath to scream. When I glanced back, They were only a few paces behind and now there were four of Them. In the distance, but not nearly far enough away, I heard the grinding of metal as the gates of hell opened and the barricades finally gave way.

I tried to go faster. I just wanted to get away, but every road I went down seemed to be full of zombies. All, it seemed, were heading towards me, with dozens more now following in my wake. I was tiring and They were getting closer.

I recognised the block I was heading down as the same one the gym was on. The entrance was around the corner. Could I get inside without Them seeing where I'd gone? Could I get inside before They caught me?

I turned the corner, reached the doorway, tore at the cord I'd tied so carefully that morning, slammed the door behind me, smacked the bolts into place, then leaned against it while looking around. How thick was that glass? I grabbed a bench and pushed it against the door. That's when the first zombie arrived. It slammed its fists against the glass. The door moved. Another arrived and pushed at the door. I grabbed and shoved every piece of furniture I could find, trying to make a barricade of my own.

Then it got worse. The banging stopped. It wasn't that They had given up, but that was when the first rush from the barricade went by. They simply swept the other zombies up into that slow, malignant wave.

They're not trying to get in, not anymore, but as this huge mass of living death makes its ponderous way past, it shoves and bangs and batters at the doors and windows. I don't know how long they will hold.

Day 37, Bermondsey, London

03:25

About an hour ago, one of the plate glass windows at the front cracked. I heard it fracture, and just, only just, managed to get a display rack in front of it before it broke. I've added some weights and one of the benches to my little barricade. I don't think the undead can get in, but They might be able to see through the gaps.

I'm sitting in the showers with the door closed and flashlight on. It's the closest to pulling the blankets over my head I could manage. It sounds like the whole of Britain north of the river, all fifty million or so, are flooding south, but it can't be. Surely it can't. Can it? And all because of me. God, I pity Sam. I pity anyone south of the river right now, anyone who gets caught outside.

It would have happened anyway. It's not my fault. The barricade just wasn't strong enough. Perhaps They didn't even see me. Probably it was just a coincidence. It's not my fault. This is not something I'm going to feel guilty about.

07:30

It's long past dawn, but there are so many of Them out there, that not even the thinnest glimmer of daylight can penetrate their ranks.

I've not really slept. There's an upstairs here, but the staircase is on the other side of the lobby. Will They see me crossing the floor?

09:00

I'm upstairs in the manager's office. I can't tell if They spotted me or not. Every few seconds, an irregular pounding will come from below as one of Them pushes at the door. Whether it's deliberate or not, I can't tell.

Fortunately there's a window up here. It's high up in the wall, near the ceiling, and from here I can see nothing except the sky, but just seeing sunlight again is soothing. Upstairs is far smaller than the ground floor, which itself isn't exactly spacious, but it feels safer. They can't get up here, not easily, and I don't think They're really trying. No. I'm safe here. Safe, for now.

I don't understand where these zombies came from. Clearly from north of the river, but where exactly? This is important. I mean really important, okay? It's not just me trying to distract myself by thinking about something else. If all of those outside were Londoners, then why didn't they leave when they were meant to? If these aren't Londoners, then what is it that, after death, drew Them to the south?

I'm trying to remember what I saw, what I *really* saw, not what I think or dread I might have seen. Were there barricades on the north bank? Tower Bridge was up. I remember that, what about Southwark Bridge? I think it was destroyed, but... no, I can't say. I couldn't see the other side of the river, couldn't say whether there were barricades there, too. All I can remember, all I can see in my mind's eye, is a sea of ghoulish faces glaring up at me.

I've seen this twice before, outside my house. One day there would be just two or three, then the next there would be dozens. A few days later, there would only be one or two again. I'd imagined that this was like a cloud moving across south London, growing as it collected more of Them in its wake, its speed and direction dictated by the obstacles in its path. Perhaps those surges were caused when other barricades, over other bridges, broke.

All right, so it doesn't matter exactly where They came from. Whether it's from London, the Midlands, or even Scotland, it doesn't really change anything, not now. Where They go, that is the more pressing question, and one for which I have no answer.

As for what I can deduce, what I actually know from what little I've seen, if I disregard those assumptions that are driven by fear, then I can say that there must have been a major outbreak during the evacuation. I'd suspected as much. Or, rather, I'd feared it.

I can picture those fenced-in roads and motorways. They were meant to keep the infected away from the evacuees, but all they did was ensure that the victims were trapped. An evacuee who'd been infected, who hoped to reach the muster point, who hoped the vaccine was a cure, died, turned, and attacked. Panic set in. People fled in both directions along the fenced-in road, not heading for safety, not heading anywhere but away. But there were too many refugees. The road would have become clogged. More were attacked. More were infected. More died. More came back, undead.

Those that still lived, with no other way of escape, would have torn down the fences. Infected and uninfected alike would have spilled out into the countryside. It can't have been long before the undead reached the next reinforced road. With hundreds or thousands of zombies now tearing at those fences, they too would give.

Perhaps that's why the barricades were thrown up. It was a hasty defence to keep the river clear while those last of the core-personnel attempted to leave. The military, the police, the hospital staff, the engineers, the politicians, Jen. Was this horde their downfall? Is this how the government fell? Are they now the dead walking the streets below? Is

115

she one of Them?

11:00

What can I do about it? Nothing. If Jen's out there, then she is. If she escaped, then she did. I can't do anything about that. I can't do anything to help her. All I can do is try to help myself, and myself needs to get out of here.

It's a small gym. Downstairs are exercise machines and weights along with changing and shower areas. Upstairs, there's a small storage area, this office, and a weird room with mats on the floor and mirrors around the edges. That gave me a shock when I opened it. I didn't recognise myself at first, covered head to toe in dirt and grime. That door is now firmly closed. At the bottom of the stairs, along with a water cooler whose contents had mostly evaporated, was the vending machine whose contents are now mostly stacked on the table.

It would have been nice if there was even one replacement water canister for the cooler, but there isn't. Judging by the stack of empty bottles by the back door they were overdue for a delivery. That's the bad news. The vending machine was half full, its contents amounting to about ten days worth of protein bars and vitamin-fortified glucose and electrolyte-enriched re-hydration fluids, or, to give it its more familiar name, squash. Add to that the energy bars, glucose tablets, and some much-welcome paracetamol in the office drawer, the boxes of vitamin tablets and body-building powder in the supply room and I'm set for a few weeks. I get the feeling that whoever ran this place might have had a side line in supplements; there's a few boxes here printed in Cyrillic, another two printed in what's possibly Chinese. Those I'll leave alone.

The towels, though. Oh, so soft and clean. If only the showers were working, I think I'd almost risk going downstairs. Almost.

For now the front doors are holding, so I'm safe, but under siege.

14:00

I moved the desk next to the window. With a chair balanced on top of it, I have a platform from which I can see outside. I can just make out the tops of their heads. The road's not as densely packed as I thought. There are only hundreds out there, not thousands. I assumed there were more, it sounded like more, perhaps because They are moving so slowly.

I've blocked the top of the stairwell. If the undead get inside, then I'm stuck here. But if They do break through my barricade, there's no way I'd make it downstairs to the back door. At least now I should be able to sleep in peace.

Day 38, Bermondsey, London

09:00

Another sleepless night, caused not from the noise, which I'm almost accustomed to, but the leg. With my eyes firmly shut, I dragged out a few of the mats from the mirror-room to sleep on, using towels for pillows and blankets. It was comfortable enough, but my leg wouldn't stop throbbing.

The exertion of the last few days has taken it out of me. Right now I can barely move, but even if I could, there's no way I could survive out there. Better to die here, of thirst.

If I'd ever had to think about what the end of the world was like, I wouldn't have imagined there would be so much boredom. All I have to read are a selection of industry magazines, sales catalogues, and one novel titled *A Cornish Daughter*. It's some kind of romantic period drama that's as bad as the name suggests. When I get out of here I'm going to keep my eyes open for some Dickens.

Day 39, Bermondsey, London

08:00

My third day in the gym, and I've been exploring my surroundings more carefully. I didn't really examine the outside of the building, but it has at least four storeys, maybe as many as six. The gym takes up a small corner unit, which means on the other side of the wall, and above my head, are other properties. I think there used to be a staircase behind a section of plasterboard in the supply cupboard. I'm not sure, but it's not like I've anything better to do than find out.

12:00

There was nothing behind the plasterboard except a cavity filled with pipes and ventilation for the showers. Going to try the walls, and see if I can break through to next door.

Day 40, Bermondsey, London

08:00

It's my fourth day here, and They are still outside, milling around, aimless, purposeless, not much different to me. That has got to change. The food I found will be gone in a week, which makes staying put suicidal, but so is going outside. I've chipped away the plaster and paint coating the walls, but the brickwork is solid, the cement relatively new. If I had time I could break through the bricks, but to what end? I can't go out. I can't go down. I can't go sideways. That only leaves up.

15:30

It took two hours to build a scaffold out of the office furniture. It seems stable enough. Balanced on top, I can reach the ceiling. Whatever is up there can't be any worse than what's outside.

Day 41, Bermondsey, London

19:00

This is almost as much fun as looting. It's exhausting, but incredibly cathartic to vent my rage and frustration on the building. I've removed the plaster, and was going to rest until the morning, but what's the point in waiting? It's not like I'm going to be able to sleep, and this may take some time.

Day 42, Bermondsey, London

05:00

Due to sheer physical exhaustion, I had to give in and sleep for a few hours. Late last night, I got a knife up between the floorboards. It went in up to the hilt so there's no carpet there. I can't hear any sounds above me, and with the racket I've been making, if there was a zombie up there, it would have heard me.

I think the zombies outside the gym heard. I think They're pushing at the doors, actually trying to get in. Peering through the window, I don't have the angle to see them, so I can't confirm it. I'm certainly not going to clear the barricade from the stairwell to check. No, I need to continue. I must keep going. Up. Up. Always up.

14:00

I'm upstairs, in the flat above the gym. I had to shift the barrier on the staircase so I could go down to the ground floor to fetch one of the long weight-bars. With that as a lever I dislodged two of the floorboards, making a space big enough to pull myself through. I pushed everything heavy I could find onto the stairwell, but I was too eager to get up and out of the gym. They saw me when I went downstairs. The sounds from the ground floor changed about half an hour after I climbed up here. I'm sure They are now in the building.

I had packed everything useful from the gym, the excess food and water, the supplements, and a few spare towels, into a couple of plastic carriers. Those were tied onto one end of a rope made from strips of towel, with the other end attached to my belt. Then I hauled myself up through the gap. That took a lot more effort than I'd expected. The cumulative effect of days of using my arms, first when walking, then to make the hole, has taken its toll.

As for up here, it's an unfurnished studio halfway through a rebuild. Sadly, the builders were beyond the stage that required the types of tools that would make a good weapon. All that's here are paint pots, brushes, and ladders. One of those would have been helpful a few hours ago.

I just re-read that. Weapons. How long since that was an everyday concern of a British citizen?

So, this is the 23rd April, day 42, and I'm not far from the broken remains of London Bridge. I have four days of food, about six litres of water. I'm in an unfinished flat with a hole in the floor. I don't know where I'm going, but I can't stay here.

17:00

If ever there was a staircase that was dark and forbidding it's the one that leads to the street. I descended far enough to make out a thin line of light surrounding the closed door before retreating back up the stairs. The other flat on the lower floor, and the ones on the top floor, are in a similar state of refurbishment to the one I climbed into. I did find a hatch leading, I hope, to an attic crawl space that will, in turn, lead to the next property. Assuming the building follows a pattern, there's a shop downstairs, next to a stairwell, next to a shop and so on, with four one-bedroom apartments split across two levels above each shop. If the undead are gathered around the gym downstairs, then there's a chance the other side of this block will be clear of Them. I'm going to rest up a bit longer, collect the ladder from downstairs, and then keep going up.

Day 43, Bermondsey, London

08:00

I got up to the attic last night, but there's barely enough light to see, let alone write. Hell, there's barely enough room to move. The only part of the floor they bothered to reinforce is the part they installed the boilers on. Boilers that are empty and still wrapped in plastic. The rest of the floor is just thin plaster and plyboard, I spent most of the night staring into the dark, balanced precariously on a beam, trying not to move.

The ladder gave me enough height to open the hatch and get halfway through. Again I'd got the bags tied to a rope the other end of which I'd tied round my waist. All was fine until I tried to pull myself up. The rope snagged on the ladder, knocking it over and down the stairs. I'd hoped I could bring the ladder with me. Getting down without it's going to be a long hard drop. But as long as I don't move, as long as I don't roll over and fall through the ceiling, I can't see any way They can reach me up here. And that's the good news.

The sound of the ladder falling echoed around the stairwell. They must have heard it. The noise from outside increased and the banging at the street door started up again. I *think* it's the street door. It sounds different to the noises I can hear from the gym, where I'm sure They are now upstairs. I could take a chance and retrieve the ladder, but could I do it without injuring myself any further? Whether I can do it without harm, there would be no way of doing it quietly. No, it's not worth the risk. More importantly it's not worth the time. Time is water, and I'm running out.

There's a thin brick wall between this property and the next. Hopefully it isn't load bearing, because today's task is to make a hole large enough to clamber through. I think the hardest part will be finding somewhere to put the bricks. Right. Break's over. Back to work.

09:45

I've made a small hole in the wall. It's just large enough to see that next door is much the same as here. There's an attic with an empty water boiler and little else. I'm taking a breather. It's not the actual job in front of me that's hard, it's the hellish contortions required so I don't fall through the thinly plastered ceiling. I'm supporting myself with my right arm and good leg while my bad leg hovers over the adjoining beam, ready to take my weight if the alternative is an ignominious fall into the room below. Ignominious? It would almost certainly be fatal. Unfortunately, balanced like this, I don't have much leverage with which to hack at the brickwork.

13:00

I'm through. It was thirsty work, though. I've already drunk the best part of a litre today. I need to be stricter.

There's an access hatch, locked from the other side. The lock doesn't bother me. What does is the idea of dropping down, finding empty flats but no ladder. I'm going to knock a small hole in the ceiling of one of the flats and see what's down there.

16:00

Both the flats are empty and unfurnished, but they have been painted. From the similarities in layout and colour scheme I think all the flats were being renovated by the same people. My hope is the next one will have been plumbed in.

I've started on the wall to the next building. If the first was Number 217, the second 215, I'm going to assume I'm now trying to break into Number 213. That's a lucky number, right?

19:30

Dinner time. One energy bar and some apple-flavoured glucose-enhanced, vitamin-enriched, mineral-drenched goop. I'm pretty sure it was originally designed as baby food before someone realised you could get an even higher mark-up by labelling it as a fitness supplement. 'N-ERvate', it's called, which has to be about the worst name going. There were only a few pouches of it in the office at the gym. It was probably a sample pack. Maybe there's a warehouse full of vats of this stuff. Hope not. It tastes as terrible as the name suggests. What I wouldn't give for a steak. Or ribs. Or a jacket potato with cheese melted on top. No, mustn't think like that. Back to the wall.

Day 44, Bermondsey, London

09:15

Lucky number 213 was finished but unfurnished. The boiler, once again, was empty. I'm not even sure it's plumbed in. I didn't bother going downstairs. Working on the next one. Number 211, I suppose. Is that lucky? I don't think so. I dropped the large water bottle. It plummeted through the ceiling. Down to one and a half bottles of lemon-flavoured sports drink, one tin of beans, and one energy bar.

17:00

Victory! Hallelujah! Rule Britannia in this Land of Hope and Glory! 211C is furnished and was, until a few months ago, lived in.

I made a small hole in the floor and checked out both flats before coming down, going so far as to put an extra hole into the bathroom ceiling just in case, but both are empty. I got down with only minimal jarring to the leg, broke the lock of the most promising door, and am now ensconced on the sofa with a bowl of cornflakes moistened with a tin of fruit salad. It wouldn't win any awards on any television cooking show, but it's about the finest thing I've ever tasted. I'm going to check out 211D in a moment. I suppose I could leave it until tomorrow. No, it's still light enough to see, this is no time to rest on my laurels.

19:00

Oh fraptious day! Rice, homemade jam, olives, gherkins, and a few more tins of fruit. Sugar packets collected from the four corners of London, and more herbs and spices than I've seen in one place, including on the stalls at a farmer's market. It's enough, more than enough. I can afford to lie low for a few days. I need some rest, after all. I deserve some. Hell, I've been stuck up in the Stygian gloom for long enough.

The jam's pretty good, the label reads 'Three Berry Jam, love, Mum'. Very good stuff. There's no mention of which three berries. I think one's got to be strawberry.

There isn't much water. There was some in the toilet cistern, but only a trickle from the boiler. I'm boiling it all up now, using a broken chair for fuel and a wok as a fire pit. I wish I'd thought of this before, it's so much more efficient than that little stove. I'll add the wok to my kit. It's heavy, sure, and unwieldy, but the grill tray fits snugly on top and the saucepan on top of that. It's all very neat.

I'm taking an evening off. I've found extra batteries so I feel like I can squander some light.

I experimented with using only one crutch, to see if that would be enough support. Unfortunately not. I was overly optimistic, I suppose. The leg needs a few more weeks. As for the cast, that's getting more ragged by the day. I've added a couple of layers of packing tape, and that should hold it together for now. What I really need is a brace of some sort, something sturdy made of metal, and then I need time to strengthen the muscles in my leg, but not tonight.

Tomorrow I'll check out the flats downstairs. Depending on what I find, I'll come up with a plan. I've enough food to stay here for a week, maybe longer, and still leave with as much as I can carry. The real limiting factor is water, but maybe I can solve that in the morning.

As to where next, having seen Them falling from the broken bridge into the Thames, the river is looking far less attractive. Certainly I wouldn't risk swimming in it, but a boat should be safe, shouldn't it? Humans float because of air in their lungs, right? And these things don't breathe, right? Except I'm sure that noise They make is caused when air accordions in and out of their lungs, so can They float, or not?

The river is close. Travelling by boat would be safer than trying to make my way south. I don't want to try walking out of London, not with however many zombies are out there now. Perhaps if I can hold out long enough, I'll be able to ride a bike straight out of the city.

Where to? Lenham Hill? Perhaps, if I can find out where that is. I'll see if I can find a map around here.

Day 45, Bermondsey, London

07:00

Up early with the lark, although for me, getting up later than six a.m. counts as a lie-in. I'm going to shop for my breakfast in the downstairs flats. Oh, wherefore art thou, bacon and eggs?

10:00

It was occupied. Only the one, I think.

14:15

They were both occupied. That explains the empty water tank. Both flats are clear now. I went as far as the street door and listened, but the undead outside don't seem to have heard the struggle.

The first one, he'd been a man once, somewhere in his twenties, though I'm basing that more on the DVD collection than on his appearance. He was in a chair when I walked in, with only the back of his head visible. At first, I thought he was alive. I actually said "hi," but as he turned, I saw his face more clearly. It was drawn, pale, almost skeletal. His bulbous eyes protruded from receding skin. On his arm was a bandage, stained brown with dried blood.

My crutches went forward. I swung in, braced myself, and brought the hammer down as the zombie tried to stand, crushing its skull in one blow.

He must have been infected, but managed to make it home. He sat down in his chair and waited to die. Did he know he was dying? Probably not. He probably thought he was the exception. It wasn't much of a view. His last sight on Earth was of a dozen anonymous and empty windows.

In the second flat were two women. Girls, really. I don't know where they came from, why they were staying here in this dingy building. There's a story, and maybe if I went through their things I could find it out. But to what end? To track down their parents to confirm their daughters are dead? Hardly.

I'd sat down, just to collect my thoughts and jot down a line or two. Writing in the journal helps to ground me, I suppose. It's a reminder that everything in this nightmare is real. The noise I made killing that first zombie must have woken the others out of their hibernating trance. They started slapping and tearing at the door, and it was clear from the noise there was more than one in there. It was the most disturbing sound I've ever heard. The door shook in its frame. I pushed against it, trying to decide what to do. Could I just walk away? It wasn't the idea of leaving them there, I've no qualms about that, but of leaving the food I'd found upstairs.

I spent too long thinking. The door gave, splitting around the hinges. I dropped the hammer as I grabbed at the wall. Off balance, trying to retain my footing, I stumbled as the first zombie fell through the doorway. She was wearing a yellow T-shirt too stained to make out the logo, and a pair of thin cotton trousers torn at the knees. Two of her fingers and four of her toes were missing. I noted that later; all I saw as she came towards me was a gaping wound where her left cheek should have been. I had the chisel, the one I use to break the locks, in my belt. I pulled it out and swung it sideways into her face. Call it luck but, in an eruption of pus and gore, it went straight through her eye socket into her skull.

I was already off-balance as the body fell towards me. I tried to push it away, and it was that effort that finally knocked me from my feet. I scrabbled backwards, away from the second of the undead women, who was now through the door and coming towards me.

126

My hands were empty. With no weapon I had no hope. I couldn't get to my feet, not without rolling onto my front, and there was no way I'd turn my back on the death that was getting inexorably closer. I crabbed backwards into the first flat. She kept following, her progress only delayed by the body of her twice dead friend lying in the hallway. My eyes darted left and right, looking for an escape, looking for a weapon, looking for something, anything that might save me from inevitable death. My gaze was always drawn back to this spectre, wearing nothing but a loose nightgown, an encrusted bandage on her arm, and an emotionless expression on her face.

I reached the coffee table, and managed to use it to pull myself to my knee. My right leg stuck out at an angle, screaming in agony. She was getting nearer, barely four steps away. I stumbled again as my leg buckled under the strain.

Three steps.

I searched behind me with my hand, my eyes fixed upon my approaching doom.

Two steps.

My fingers found something.

One step.

I brought my arm up in a roundhouse swing. With the object I'd found gripped tightly in my hand, there was enough force to knock her from her feet. After she hit the floor, there was barely a pause before she tried to get back up. I crawled forward, my leg dragging behind, reaching her as she rolled over onto her front. I brought the weight down on the back of her knee, crushing the bone. I dragged myself forward and brought the weight down on her spine. With each upswing I pulled myself forward and brought the weight down, crushing bone and pulping flesh. All that time, her hands and feet twitched. Her jaw snapped as she tried to get up, tried to turn, tried to bite and tear at me. I was sobbing, crying, screaming, and then I was at her head. I brought the weight down on her skull. Twice. Only then did I look and see what was in my hands. It was a metal moneybox in the shape of a London bus.

Day 46, Bermondsey, London

11:00

I stripped off on the stairs. Even forgetting the potential for infection, those clothes are unwearable. I've washed all over with a bottle of peroxide I found in the upstairs flat. That should be strong enough to kill any... any germs. I hope. It'll have to do. It was all I could find.

Four flats, three infected, one survivor got away. It was the one whose mother sent the jam. That makes sense. Why else leave all this food, unless you knew that They were in the flats beneath you? Someone got away. That thought is all that's holding me together right now.

It was the sight of all those little jars of jam, all signed 'love, Mum'. I don't know if I could handle the idea that one of the zombies I'd just killed was their owner. I know it's too late for a cure. Even so, I wonder how many of Them, even if there was a cure, if They were brought back to us right now, how many of Them would want to?

12:30

I've new clothes once again. They're the wrong size, but who cares about that. A pair of scissors took care of most of my hair, and the rest, I guess the peroxide will turn it blond and that'll be my new look for this new age. It's not the same as having a long, hot shower, but it's helped. I'd like, and had been hoping, to say that I feel like a new person. Except I don't.

My leg's throbbing, it's a dull persistent ache, and that's after I've taken two of the painkillers. I guess it's been like that for days, but it's been considerate enough to wait until now to let me know. It'll probably heal, probably badly. I doubt I'll ever run again. No more guilt-laden, morning-after jogging for me!

As for the cast, it's covered in grime, I'm not even going to begin to describe it, but until I can find a replacement it has to stay on.

No flies. That's interesting, isn't it? There were no flies in the flats. If this was a movie, then when I went into that first flat, there should have been a swarm of insects around the body. There were scores of insects around the driver of the government car. What was it about this body that repelled the insects? Does it mean that They are not really decaying? That, as the fluids evaporate, They are becoming desiccated? I don't want to think about that and what it means. Not now. Not today.

I went downstairs. I had to check the apartments for food so I could calculate how long I can stay here, how long I can sleep. There's enough for a few weeks. Maybe longer. Enough that I don't need to count too precisely.

I guess that's to be expected. The people who left with the evacuation were the ones who had to, the ones who had no supplies left. They had been the people who queued for hand-outs at the supermarkets. The people who stayed, they were the ones who bought food in bulk for financial, cultural, or dietary reasons, or because they simply hated shopping. There had been a lot, in both apartments, or a lot for an apartment this size, but the tenants had stayed here a long time before they became infected. A kilo of rice, seven tins of tuna, a couple of packs of crackers, some noodles, and an assortment of tins whose contents I'm going to have to guess on based on the pictures since the labels aren't printed in English.

I can stay here a fortnight, if I can find the water to cook with. I used up the last of what was in the toilet cisterns for rinsing off after my peroxide sponge-bath. That leaves two litres of Coke, one of lemonade, and one of something pink that's either alcoholic or drain cleaner.

It rained last night. Not heavily. Just enough to splatter the windows. That's going to be the long-term solution to the water situation. I just need to work out how to collect it. Not today. For now, I'm going to sleep.

Day 47, Bermondsey, London

06:30

Coke for breakfast, in lieu of coffee. Not quite the same. Ooh, I've an idea!

07:10

I boiled up some Coke to make cola-flavoured coffee. Or is it coffee-flavoured cola? I'm calling it colaffee, and if I'm honest, I'd have to say it tastes better than that pink stuff.

I'm feeling far more upbeat this morning. No. Not upbeat, just more accepting, I suppose. Have decided to have a day off. Who needs water when you have colaffee?

19:00

Something has been nagging at me over the last few days, but I suppose I've not had the luxury to really think about it until now. I'm hoping putting it down on paper will help clarify my thoughts.

It's the driver. The one Jen sent, or at least the one I thought she sent. Did she actually send him? That's what's bugging me. I didn't speak to her, and the only reason I thought he'd come at her behest was the text message I received. Or, to be more precise, the one sent from her phone.

She spent three weeks resolutely keeping me away from the evacuation, and for reasons I can't begin to fathom, keeping me away from wherever she was. Jen and I are family. Or as close to family as I've got, so when she sent someone to collect me, why was it someone I didn't know? When he didn't return, why didn't she follow up? And why *was* he on his own? She knew I couldn't walk. Since it took two of them to get me up to the flat, how was one of them going to get me down? Why was there no wheelchair? Why was he fitting a silencer to a gun, one he didn't keep on his person where it would be ready to hand?

Maybe there wasn't a wheelchair to spare, and it's not like I'd need one for a car journey. Fine, I can accept that, but if she was in a position to send a car with its priceless fuel, surely she could spare a couple of people. It wasn't like human beings were in short supply.

All right, Mr Paranoid, what is it you're suggesting? What is it that's been eating away at you? Well, I'll tell you. The silencer. Why would you fit one of those to a gun? Well, yes, obviously so that no one else would hear the shot, and yes, that could be an issue with the undead. Next to the sound of a car engine, however, the sound of a single shot fired at a zombie close enough to hit with a handgun isn't a risk worth worrying about. No, the only reason I can think why the gun would be in the glove box, at a time when even the police were armed, was if you didn't want anyone to know you had it. The only reason you'd fit a silencer to a gun would be if you didn't want other people, other living people, to hear the shot.

Jen knew that my tenants had left, but that doesn't mean she'd told anyone else. The Radio Free England people said that the government had fallen, but which government did it mean? Who were these men working for that she felt she couldn't speak freely to me in their presence?

But why does that matter? The evacuation clearly failed. Knowing who and why someone was sent to kill me doesn't help in getting out of here, but perhaps it alters my destination.

20:00

In the last two weeks I've killed, if that's the right word, five people. I've let loose, albeit unwittingly, thousands of the undead into south London, thus indirectly endangering and probably killing an unknown number of survivors. I've broken into four flats, one gym and one shop, looted, stolen, caused criminal damage, and I plan to cause more. I shouldn't feel guilty about any of this, but I do.

I was worried that some of the blood, or gore, or whatever that brownish ooze They have under the skin is, might have seeped under the cast and into some unseen scratch or graze on my leg. I didn't want to say anything, didn't want to write it down, in case the act itself in some way made it more real. Call it superstitious if you want, but look outside the window and tell me this isn't a world made for superstition. Eight o'clock tonight was my cut-off point. If I got this far, then I knew I wasn't infected. Well, it's eight o'clock and I'm not infected. No, I'm just lucky. I never believed in luck before and find it hard to believe now.

There are hundreds milling around outside. They're all heading vaguely westward except by the door to the gym. There's about a dozen by the front doors. I'm not sure how many are inside, but if I were to guess, based on the gym's layout and the way the undead around the door are moving, I would say that there are maybe twenty inside.

Sometimes one of the undead slouching along the street will stop and join those trying to get inside. Sometimes one of those at the doors will be jostled or knocked far enough away that They drift off and rejoin the exodus. It's like magnetism, in a way. Or gravity. There's a certain distance from the gym at which the mass of the herd becomes more desirable than, well, than me.

I have no idea what the significance of this is. Something to do with pack mentality, or hive minds, or scent, or senses, or I don't know what. I think if I observe Them I'll learn more about Them, but what more do I need to know?

I didn't have a plan for what to do if I *knew* I was infected. Suicide would be an option, but I can't really see the point since I'd be dead either way. I suppose I'm just like that guy downstairs, thinking I'm somehow different.

Day 48, Bermondsey, London

09:00

I've three weeks of food, which I can probably stretch to a very hungry four. I've only a few days of fluids left. I've come up to the attic to see how difficult it would be to knock a hole in the roof through which I could collect rainwater. Very difficult, is the answer. There's not enough room to stand up straight, and nothing but the joists with which to support myself. After twenty minutes of contortions, I found a position from which I could reach the roof, but it's too solidly built. Given time, I could break through, but I don't know if I have that long. Besides, it's not raining. That leaves me with little choice but to break through to the next set of flats and hope I find water in there.

15:00

Not a good day. I broke through to number 209. From the attic I could hear movement below. I made a small hole in the ceiling and peered down. I saw nothing. I moved to where I thought the bathroom would be and made another hole. Still nothing. I crawled to the opposite side of the attic and checked the other flat, but it too was empty. The noises, I thought, must be coming from the downstairs flats.

If it, or They, were making that much noise, then there had to be a reason. Perhaps someone else was down there. That made me hesitate for a few moments until I realised that if I could hear it from up here, then those creatures outside would be able to hear it, too. I was far more concerned about the noise than about the potential for companionship. I guess that's something to do with Sam, or perhaps it's just that I've survived so long on my own. Either way, that noise had to stop. It was bad enough having Them in the gym at that end of the building. If the undead congregated outside this end as well, I might end up truly trapped with no way out.

This time, I was better prepared. I'd donned extra layers, even over the cast. The only part of my body not covered was around my eyes. I'd brought the ladder up to the attic with me, so getting down only entailed opening the hatch, lowering the ladder, and hopping down one rung at a time.

Preparation can only take you so far. I made too much noise. I should have wrapped the ladder in cloth or something, anything to stop it banging and clattering as I tried to manoeuvre it in such a small space. Eventually the ladder was in place, my good leg was on the top rung, my bad one hung in mid-air. That's when I realised the heaving wheeze was getting closer. It wasn't coming from inside the flat. It was coming up the stairs. There was no time to go back up. I had to get down and face it.

Foot down, drop. Foot down, drop. I was too slow. Twisting my head,

I saw it. I know it was just a trick of the light, but I swear its eyes glowed with a predatory glee. It lunged. I swung the crutch, knocked the zombie off balance, and dropped down one more rung. The creature lunged again. Still on the ladder, I twisted, balancing on my good leg, and lanced the crutch straight at its head. There wasn't much power to the blow, but the zombie's own momentum did most of the work. It pivoted, fell, and landed on its back. With so much cloth padding on the crutch, I'd done no damage. As soon as it was down, it tried to get back up. All that saved me was that it couldn't seem to work out whether to roll onto its right side or onto its left.

I dropped down one more rung. I was three feet from the landing. I jumped the rest of the way, hopping and twisting to face the zombie. Now that I was closer, it stopped trying to roll and started thrashing its arms. I knocked them out of the way with the crutch, stepped forward, and brought down the hammer. It died.

I was breathing so hard, it sounded like it was in stereo. Then I realised that it wasn't me. There were two more coming up the stairs.

A memory flashed across my mind of childhood summers when Jen and I visited medieval castles. I remembered being told how the spiral staircases were designed so the right-handed defenders could use their swords to full effect. All those interminable tours and unbelievable re-enactments came back to me as I watched the first zombie half-crawl, half-walk its way up the stairs. I pushed at it with the crutch, knocking it off balance, and back into the creature behind. I suppose if I'd been facing living people wearing twice their bodyweight in metal armour, this would have been a good strategy. As it was, the fall did Them no obvious damage. I just had to wait while They disentangled themselves and resumed their laborious climb.

I couldn't reach the zombie while it was on the stairs, flailing its arms. I had to step back and wait until it reached the landing. Hands, then forearms, then elbows slapped onto the top-most step. Thrashing its legs, it stretched out an arm towards me. I pushed the crutch down on its shoulders, pinning it before slamming the hammer down on its skull. With the crutch, I levered the corpse down the stairs, toppling the third zombie back to the landing. That gave me another minute to catch my breath while that last creature slowly climbed towards me. Again, I stepped back, waiting until it had reached the top-most step, waiting until it began to stand, waiting until its head tilted up before I smashed the hammer down.

Finally, it was over. I waited, my body tense in case there were more, but I could hear nothing beyond that infernal scuffling from outside.

I had to check the flats. I mean, it was clear these were the former residents. They were just wearing normal clothes, not the kind you'd expect if they'd been outside and sought refuge here. But first I had to make sure my escape route was clear. I'd learned my lesson, you see. I checked the ladder was secure, then pushed the two bodies to the top of the stairs. It wasn't much of a barricade, but good enough to give me a little time while I went inside the flats. There was nothing there. No undead, no food, no water.

I pushed the bodies to one side then went downstairs. One room was locked. From the bloodstains on furniture and floor, the other was where at least one of the people had turned. I turned my attention to the locked door. My arms were tired, and my entire body ached, so it took a little effort and a lot of time, but I finally managed to get the door open.

On a small bedside was an empty glass and an equally empty pill bottle. On the bed was the body of a young man. In his dead hands was a letter. It read:

"To whom it may concern.

My name is Tamotso Yoshida, from Kyoto, Japan. I came to England to continue my studies in applied fluid dynamics at King's College London. I am twenty-seven years old.

I rented this flat through an agency provided by the university. Beyond an occasional nod of greeting, I did not know the other tenants. We met properly on the first day of the curfew. I returned from the laboratory to discover them huddled around the front door. With no shops open they had no reason to go out, but they were too terrified to stay in their apartments.

We didn't bond. We weren't friends. We never entirely trusted one another, but we agreed to stay together, to pool our resources, to help each other survive. We went to the university, broke into the coffee shop, and stole all we could carry. It wasn't much, but enough, we thought, for a month. By then the crisis would be over.

We decided not to leave when we were ordered to. The conditions the evacuees would face would, at best, be unsanitary, but it was more likely it would be lethal. There is no way the government can ensure the infected won't be among those joining the evacuation. There simply are not the resources to examine everyone.

It was this argument that persuaded the others to stay, but I do not accept responsibility for their decision. It was theirs alone. They wanted to stay. They felt safe here. It was their choice.

We went out in search of food. We broke into houses and shops and took whatever we could find. It was never more than we could carry. At first it was terrifying, then it was thrilling, but that faded as more of the undead appeared on the streets.

When the electricity was cut off, we started to worry. When the water stopped flowing, Kashandra wanted to go outside, to get more supplies. I did not. I wanted to wait. We had enough to last for weeks. We voted. I lost. She and Max left early on Saturday morning. There were no undead outside. Not then.

They were gone for three hours, and returned empty handed and silent. I knew something was wrong. But they would not say any more than they had been unsuccessful.

Kashandra developed a fever around two p.m. By three, she was unconscious. At four, she died. A minute later, she came back and attacked Max. I ran from the room into here, where we'd stored our food. I closed the door in Talil's face. He hammered at the door. I ignored him, ignored his screams as they killed him. Ignored him when he came back and hammered at the door once more.

Now the food is gone, and I am down to the last glass of water.

This is not death. It is peace. Good bye."

16:30

Who am I to judge him? Would I have done any differently? I'd like to think I'd have fought, but how long did I stay in my house, all locked up and safe? If I'd still had enough of those little blue pills when I was trapped in the gym, or when I thought I'd been infected, I might have made the same decision as he did. No, it isn't for me to judge him or anyone else.

I've run out of water. All I have left is the last bottle of Coke. I've taken a look around, but there isn't anything here, not even clean clothes. I put the letter on the bedside table and pulled the door closed. Perhaps someone will come looking for him one day, but I doubt it.

19:00

The wall sealing the attic in Tomotso's flat with the next one is much thicker, at least three bricks deep, with fresh-looking cement. I've just spent an hour working at it and only managed to remove two bricks. At this rate I'll die of dehydration before I break through, and then what? I can't risk finding nothing on the other side. Instead, tomorrow, I'm going out the front door.

I've brought everything useful, but which I can't carry, up to the attic space, and I'm going to take the door key with me. It comes to at least three weeks of food. There's no guarantee I'll be able to get back in, but I like the idea of somewhere to fall back to.

I can't work out if I've had mostly good luck so far, or mostly bad.

Day 49, Bermondsey, London

16:00

Either They are getting slower or I'm getting faster. I'm sure it's the latter. I didn't have to kill any of Them today. Then again, I'm only a few hundred yards from where I started and the day is far from over.

They didn't notice me at first. I had time to close the door to the flats and maybe, just maybe They didn't spot where I was coming from. Maybe that flat will still be safe if I need to go back. Maybe the undead don't care where I came from. Surely that requires more reasoning than They are capable of. I only managed twelve paces from the door before I was spotted and the chase began.

We can manage about the same speed, Them and me. By the time I'd reached the junction, the zombies from the side of the building had spotted me. It became quickly apparent that I'd no chance of outpacing Them.

I know glancing behind is meant to slow you down, or maybe that's only for sprinters, but I had to look. I wish I hadn't. There were scores of gaping, snarling mouths pursuing me, all with the same terrible purpose. I knew, out in the open, They would catch me. Without the time to select a refuge, I headed to this building site. It's the was-soon-to-open-but-now-never-will Havingdon Estate. The builder's hoarding promised a mixture of prime retail and premium housing in one of the country's most desirable locations. In reality, it was going to be just another generic block of flats with shops underneath. They got as far as putting in the foundations, the lift-shafts, and four of the floors, but not the plumbing, walls, windows, or doors.

The padlock on the entrance had already been broken. A chain looped around the door kept it closed. Clearly someone else has been here. Whoever that was, they left no trace of where they went.

I'm on the second floor of a small, low building off to one side of the main construction site. It's become my fortress for the night, and it's a good one. There was a scaffolding walkway between it and the next building, and no other way to get up here. I've pulled the walkway back. Even if the undead get into the site, I can pull the walkway across, position it on the other side, balance it on the fence, and sort of drop down to the street below.

Okay, it doesn't sound like a great plan, not written down like that, but it is. What makes me certain are the scorch marks on the concrete, and the group of trunnions. They are called trunnions, aren't they, these metal hooks embedded in the concrete to which the walkway can be attached?

No, maybe they're called something else, I can't remember.

Someone went to a lot of work in preparing an escape route. All I need to do is attach the walkway and push it forward, gravity will do the rest, and I've got a ramp to walk down. More of a slide, I suppose, and there'll be a drop at the bottom. Won't be able to get back up here afterwards, but that's okay.

I've made a splint out of some lengths of aluminium, gaffer tape, and electrical wire, and strapped it over the cast. I have to be careful with the leg now. Something scrapes inside when I try to move it. As long as I don't panic, I think I'll be able to outpace Them. Yes, yes, I will. I'm certain of it. I've been practising up here. There's not much space, only fifteen steps from one edge to the other, but that's more than I had in the flat. I'm good to go. Just need to wait for Them to disperse a bit, I've just got to wait. Yes. All in all, a good day.

Hope it rains. Best not to think about it, I suppose. I should think about something else. What, though?

This is the first time I've seen a group of Them up close. At home, They were always in that sort of torpid state. When I was in the gym, and from the flats above, I couldn't see much of the streets below. On the Web, the distance afforded by the screen kept me removed from the reality of what I was seeing.

There are a couple of bodies out there, killed, I assume, by whoever sought refuge here before me. Who were they? When did they leave? How far behind them am I? As to why they left, that's clear enough. This is a good place to defend as long as you have supplies, but without them, without anything to burn, with no real shelter against the elements, with no water to drink… No. I mustn't think about that.

Where did they go? It's not that I want company, you understand. I mean, it'd be nice, one day, when all this has settled down, but I'm coping okay on my own. I got this far alone, didn't I? Other people would just slow me down. Too many arguments, too many compromises. I've a plan; as long as I stick to it, I'll be fine.

Very thirsty. It's cold up here and there's nothing to burn. I should have packed some firewood. I could burn this journal. No, this is my link with... with sanity, I suppose. Besides it wouldn't keep me warm for more than a few seconds.

They're not really pounding at the door. They're trying to reach through it. The banging is as often caused by their heads as it is by their hands. And those hands aren't knocking with the knuckles or slapping with the palm like I would. No, They are clawing and pawing at it, as if They can't understand why this great impediment is between Them and their prey. I suppose They can't understand, can They?

How many calories do the undead burn doing that? How long before their bodies are exhausted? It can't be long. I can't imagine They actually eat their victims, not eat and digest, I mean.

Are these zombies decaying, or just desiccating as I feared? It's still too early to tell. Some look far more ragged than others, but I don't think it's decay. I think it's just that They aren't healing. Open wounds widen as movement tears the skin and muscles apart. That doesn't slow Them down much. I suppose this explains the torpid state when They rest on their haunches and hibernate, or whatever it is.

Time. That's what I need. Time to rest. Time to outlast Them. I need to find somewhere safe for a few months. Somewhere with water. Maybe until the end of summer, then I'll need food for the winter. That'll be the tough one. Which direction to go, though? The river's to the north, not far to the north either, and that's about the only direction that there isn't any smoke. Everywhere else, south, east, and west, and across the river, pillars of smoke dot the skyline. I could go back to the house, I suppose. It's not far, and the car's there. So is that gun. I don't know if the car would still work, but the gun surely would. Surely. No, that's going back. But if not there, then where?

Buckingham Palace? There'll be food for thousands of people for a decade or more, plus a fire suppression system that's bound to work even in a power cut. Trouble is, so is the alarm system. It'd be just my luck to get that far and find bars over the gates and windows. No. Besides it's on the wrong side of the river. It's the same with the Tower of London. I can almost see it from here. It'd make a great place for a stand-off. After all, it was built as a proper castle, wasn't it? But the Tower is also north of the river and unlike Buck Pal it wouldn't have any stores.

They've stopped banging at the door. It's half-past five. That's sooner than I'd have expected. I'm going to investigate.

19:15

Half of the zombies have already wandered off. The other half are milling around the door to the building site, acting as if They can't decide whether to continue pursuing me, or to follow the others. I slid the walkway back onto the main building and have climbed up to the fourth floor, that's as high as the ramps go. I'm not going to risk the ladders.

The zombies that left are heading towards a building to the south of here. It's about half a mile away, maybe less than that. A third of a mile? I wish I had a map.

That building is completely surrounded by Them, five or six deep, and not just around the front, but the sides as well. There's only one reason They are there, but I don't think I can do anything to help.

Day 50, Surrey Quays, London

15:00

I'm saying a prayer of thanks to whichever sainted politician allowed vending machines inside schools. I'm sitting in the Business and Innovation Centre at St Miriam's Academy, gorging myself on sun-dried tomato bites and cartons of genuine fruit juice.

I took a detour inland to avoid the Rotherhithe Tunnel and whatever horrors dwell inside it. Perhaps they blew it up, but perhaps they didn't.

I finally got a view of the river today. A proper view, and as far as I could see, there were no floating zombies. There's a lot of detritus in the water, but I think that the river's safe.

In the end, I decided to give that building to the south with all the zombies outside a wide berth. Last night, I thought a lot about what I could do to help. Starting a fire was the only thing I could think of, but that wouldn't distract the undead. Besides, I had nothing to burn.

In the end I did nothing. That's not as callous a decision as it sounds. I think that whoever's in there must realise that noise attracts Them. If those survivors stayed quiet for a day or two, the undead would disperse, and they could escape. That they haven't suggests that whatever noise they are making is deliberate. Perhaps they have plenty of food, and are trying to gather the undead there to make it easier for others. Perhaps. I hope so. I couldn't see a way to help them then, and I can't think of one now.

The best find here has to be toilet paper and an unblocked toilet. I can't flush it, but I don't plan on staying here long. It's the simple things in life...

Some schools tried to open the morning after New York. Many others couldn't, as staff refused to come in. They were all shut while I was in the hospital. It wasn't that they worried about their being an outbreak at a school. These days, with their double-locked security gates, schools are as secure as a prison. If there was an outbreak at a school, it would be easily contained. There was a plan for that. As far as I know, that plan was never implemented, at least not at a school.

The day after I was released from the hospital, a plane from LAX tried to land at Heathrow. It wasn't a scheduled flight. A USAF colonel had led a mixture of full-timers, reservists, and their families to the airport. They broke in, stole a plane, took off, and flew east with two hundred souls aboard.

There was almost a happy ending. The colonel knew the right frequencies. He'd warned London he was coming, and we were willing to accept him. He hadn't said there was at least one infected person on board. He was smart, or smart enough to wait until he was approaching the capital before he told air traffic control. By then it was too late to shoot down the aircraft. He must have known at least some of his passengers were infected even if they hadn't yet turned. He'd kept his family with him in the cockpit and they, he assured the tower, were clean. That wasn't good enough.

They used the plane as an experiment. A way of testing different nerve agents to see what worked on the undead. Jen told me that not many did, which tallied with the reports from the countries where we'd got those weapons in the first place.

The point is that we... no. *They*, the government, not me, *they* were ready to take out a school if it was necessary. The real risk wasn't in having to sanitise a school. It was the danger that, having unleashed a chemical weapon on a school, a conscientious journalist might report it. Then we'd have ended up with the riots they had in Japan.

How did I feel about learning that my erstwhile colleagues had devised and were prepared to implement a plan to kill school children if they felt it might halt the outbreak? I can't even think of a single historical precedent for such actions. I can blame the painkillers, the pain itself, or just the whole psychological disconnect everyone must have felt when they found themselves in a living nightmare, but maybe it goes deeper than that. How *did* I feel? I didn't care. And now? I think I feel differently. It's hard to say. I'm so emotionally drained, so tired, so on edge, I don't know what it means to be human anymore beyond that basest, simplest desire to live. No, I do feel differently. I'm sure of that, though I'm not sure who I am, or who I was, or how much I've changed.

Too much introspection. Too much remembering the past. I should just be grateful for something to eat, something to drink, and somewhere safe to sleep. And toilet paper. I'm grateful for that, one more thing I didn't think to include in my pack. Two rolls now have pride-of-place at the top of the bag where they'll be easy to reach. Double-wrapped in carrier bags, of course, because there's nothing worse in my little world than soggy toilet paper!

Now, there's a thought. Maybe the art room will have some plaster of Paris, or whatever the modern-day equivalent is. Surely there'll be something. I'm off to investigate.

143

Day 51, New Cross, London

05:00

The school was infested. That's a good word for it. Infested. One almost got me. Almost. It was breathing into my face. I spent all night worried that it had spat some of its saliva or whatever into my mouth, or nose, or eyes. It can't have, though. I mean, I'm still here, right? Yeah. Lucky again.

There were twelve of the undead, that's how many chased me. They weren't old. I mean, They were newly turned. Their ages before, I'd have to put at between twenty and thirty, maybe a little older but not much. They didn't appear dried out and desiccated the way some of the others do.

At least one of them must have worked in the school because the doors were unlocked. I should have noticed that.

I was looking for the art supply room. The only floor plans of the school I found listed the classrooms, but not the subjects that were taught in them. Instead, I looked for the building with the most student art on the wall, hoping that was a logical place to start my search.

The ground floor had nothing but rooms filled with chairs and tables, and no sign of any supply cupboards. I went upstairs, and found a classroom that had a promising collection of pottery on the windowsill and a likely-looking door at the back.

I heard it before I got to the second row of desks, not coming from the supply room, but from behind me, from the door I'd just entered. Slowly, I turned around. As quietly as I could, I let go of the crutch and pulled out the hammer. I inched forward. I could hear it, and it wasn't getting any closer, but nor was it getting further away. I decided to make a run for it.

Gingerly, I stepped out into the corridor. I saw it on the other side of the fire doors, about ten yards from me. Our eyes met. It snarled and staggered along the corridor towards me. I hurriedly stepped back into the classroom. I didn't know if fire doors could be locked, and what would happen when it hit the plastic windows. I *hoped* they were locked. They weren't, and the windows weren't made of plastic. It ran straight into the plate glass and kept going, over the banister and down into the stairwell, landing in a twisted gory heap about halfway up.

I followed the creature down the stairs, not sure if it was still alive. Its body was punctured by jagged shards, but that's not enough to kill one of Them. It writhed, its grunting hiss and moan punctuated by the crunch of glass as it tried to stand. A flailing arm caught the crutch, knocking it from my grasp. I was unbalanced. I slipped. I fell, landing on the stairs, three steps up from it. Slivers of glass bit into my skin as the zombie crawled towards me. I kicked at the zombie, pushing it away with my foot, until I had enough room to stand. Then I swung the hammer again and again and again, until it finally stopped moving.

I was sure I'd been infected. I fell to my knees, screaming. That's why I didn't hear the others. Three faces appeared at the top of the stairwell. I pushed myself to my feet, limped out of the building, and out of the school.

I kept moving for the rest of the day and into the night. Sometimes I lost some of Them, sometimes I picked up more. I finally escaped by leading Them up the ramp to the roof of a multi-storey car park, speeding up when I got to the top so They didn't see me when I ducked into the stairwell. When I finally got out of that car park and headed out into the street below, the zombies left on the top floor spotted me. They started pushing and shoving until the safety barrier broke and They plunged down, one after another, sixty feet to the pavement.

I was exhausted, and convinced I was already dead. I barely had the energy to climb up a ladder to the flat roof of this petrol station. I didn't sleep.

I picked out six fragments of glass from my skin. Six! And I didn't get infected. That's not just luck, that's something else. From now on, no more risks. All I want is somewhere quiet to hide for a few months. Somewhere where this will all just stop.

Day 52, Woolwich, London

06:00

Finally. Safety. I'm in a house to the north of Woolwich, a few hundred metres from the Thames. It's a nice house, a late Victorian family place with five bedrooms, a plethora of bathrooms, and a massive open-plan living-room-kitchen. I've always fancied one of those. There's a working fireplace, too. The original mantelpiece has been replaced with something distinctly Scandinavian, but I'm not going to complain about that.

There are lots of houses in this neighbourhood, packed almost one on top of the other, but there's a lot of greenery, too. Lots of trees and large gardens. I found the house last night, and after I'd checked it was empty, I collapsed on the sofa and didn't move until dawn.

The fire's lit, and writing in the journal is only delaying the inevitable. It's time for the cast to come off.

09:00

What a stench!

I'd boiled some water from the water-butt in the garden. It's a stagnant greenish colour, and there's no way I'm going to drink it. Perhaps washing my leg with it wasn't a good idea either. Still, like the old saying goes, "When the dead walk the Earth…"

As for the leg, well, it's a mix of the disgustingly pale, the rubbed raw, and the dirt-engrained, but it's still there and it still works. I've strapped it up as best I can with electrical tape and the supports from a shelving unit. It's not perfect, and far from ideal, but it seems to hold.

10:00

On second inspection there is no way I'm reusing the water-butt. It's caked with a greenish slime that seems to be making a run at becoming humanity's replacement as this planet's dominant life form. I've chucked out the rest of the water I boiled up. I really don't want to risk getting sick.

First order of business, I suppose, is to find a new water barrel.

12:00

Some pasta for lunch, cooked in wine. I couldn't find anything else. Makes the pasta almost look like there's a sauce with it. There had been more food here, packets of some kind, but mice got in at some point. Anything not in glass or plastic has gone. They've even chewed through the labels on the few tins that remained.

I couldn't find a proper rain barrel, but then what was I expecting, that there would be a spare, still in its sterilised wrapping hidden in a back room? That would have been nice. The largest of the saucepans is currently doing duty instead. Even that, I think, is optimistic. When did it last rain? A week ago?

Now that I think about it, I'm going to need more firewood. The owners had laid a fire, but I think they only used it for decoration. I filled the house with smoke before I found the lever to open the flue. I suppose I could always burn the furniture, but I don't like the idea of that. I mean, this is someone's home, someone who may plan on coming back some day. I know, I know, I've already been burning books and furniture, but that was in my house. It was my furniture, and those books were all mass-produced, all replaceable, not dog-eared from years of reading and re-reading. As for the flats above the gym, I know that none of those occupants cared any more.

I've taken down the photographs. I couldn't stand looking at the school portraits, holiday snaps, and the family pictures where they're all standing by the Christmas tree. Everyone is always smiling, even when the smile never reaches the eyes. I've not hidden them. I just laid the frames down so the faces aren't staring at me, aren't judging me.

I wonder if they made it, if they survived. I know they planned their escape, you can tell they'd packed and re-packed by the mess in the kid's room. There was only the one child still at home. The other two, about a decade older, must have moved out or been at university. Are they on a ship? Maybe they're already at work in some field somewhere, turning a grass pitch into farmland. They'll be thinking about this house and all the

147

happy times they had here, and about the times they'll have here again, when it's all over.

One day someone will come back to reclaim their possessions. It might not be the parents. It might be the children, grown up, or even their children. Someday, someone will come for the photographs of their mother sitting in the chair by the fire. There are three different photographs, each taken years apart. Though her hair changes and there are more lines on her face, in each picture she has the same look of joy in her eyes.

Perhaps they won't come back, but if they do I can't have them finding the house has been ransacked, that there's no trace left of their old lives. I couldn't live with that. Not now. Not anymore.

Yesterday I found a different house, belonging to a different family, a family who hadn't left. Mother, Father, and two children.

It was the first time I'd seen an undead child, seen one properly, I mean. There were some in the crowds outside my house, but I didn't look, didn't *see*. I mean, I was never that close. All right, maybe I avoided looking too hard, but there must have been dozens, hundreds, thousands even, in the horde that swept by the gym. I didn't notice. I chose not to notice.

I lost my bag, one of the crutches, and the hammer in that house. It's only around the corner, just a couple of blocks from here, but I'm not going back.

By midday, yesterday, I'd reached Greenwich. That's a distance of a mile or so as the crow flies, but I'd travelled a lot further. I kept circling around to the river, looking for anything that might float. I'd scaled my dreams back from houseboat to launch to dinghy to anything that might take me out with the tide. There was nothing but broken wood and plastic. The spots where the river taxis used to dock had been broken down, the piers now stubs of broken timber against the banks.

It wasn't easy. There were still scores of the undead on the streets. Sometimes I could sneak by unseen, sometimes I had to double back, sometimes I had to run, sometimes I had to kill. Once, I had to break through the plate glass of an estate agent's window and escape down the alley behind the shop to evade fifteen of Them. After that, I finally abandoned the idea of fleeing by river. Instead I set my sights on somewhere to hide up for a day or three. I turned away from the Thames and wandered the side roads, my route determined by where the undead were least concentrated. That's when I saw the house. It wasn't hard to spot, it was the only house I'd seen with the windows newly boarded up. Someone *had* been there and, I thought, might be there still.

I knocked on the door. There was no answer. I knocked again, this time more rhythmically, trying to make it clear that I was one of the living. Still, there was no answer. I thought that they'd either fled, or perhaps gone foraging. The door was locked but not barred, which suggested the latter. Carefully, not wanting to cause too much damage, I levered the door open. It'd be easy to repair, I thought, and I didn't want to wait out on the street, not where I could be spotted.

I stepped inside. It took a moment for my eyes to adjust to the gloom. The noise of my knocking must have woken her. The mother stood just inside the door, and was almost on top of me when I opened it. I pushed her flailing arms aside, brought the hammer up, and slammed it down on her skull.

I closed the door behind me, and pushed the body out of the way. I could have left then, but thought if she was the only one, then that house might make a good place to rest for a few days. The father appeared at the end of the hallway, the remains of a bandage visible on his neck. He must have been the first one infected. He'd managed to make it home before he turned. I killed him quickly, too quickly, too easily. It's becoming too easy.

The rest of the house was silent. I walked through the hall, towards the kitchen. I was maybe halfway there when I realised there was something behind me. Maybe it was a sound, maybe a sixth sense. I mean, something has got me through this so far, right?

I turned around. Two girls stood there. One was maybe six, the other a few years older. Mouths agape, clothing stained with their own dried blood, they walked slowly towards me. I couldn't do it. For each of us there's a line we just will not cross, and for me, that was the line.

Why didn't we just tell everyone to stay inside and wait for the vaccine? That makes far more sense than some trek into the middle of nowhere. Those children would have lived.

I pushed through them and ran out the front door.

They might have died anyway, but they would have had a chance.

They followed me out of the house. I lost them in the next block when, once more, I hid in the bushes of an overgrown front garden. I lay there for hours, not thinking, not doing anything. When it started to get dark I crawled round to the back of the property. I couldn't face going inside, couldn't face the idea of having to deal with anything else that night, so I lay there, under the stars, trying to forget their faces.

Finally, I got up. The road was empty. I walked stiffly across the street, broke the side gate, and made my way into the back garden where I made a hole in the fence. I had enough energy to get inside this house and check it was empty before I fell asleep.

17:00

I'm feeling tired. It's been a long couple of days. I think I'll give up on any plans more long-term than waking up tomorrow morning.

There were twelve bottles of mineral water in the cellar. That's more than enough for now. Never made tea with mineral water before.

Day 53, Woolwich, London

Sick.

Day 59, Woolwich, London

09:00

Something I ate, something I drank, too much stress or something worse, who knows? Maybe it was something in the air. Whatever it was, it resulted in vomiting and diarrhoea, and I'll leave the descriptions there. I'm slightly better today, though I feel weaker than ever.

I heard birdsong this morning, louder than I've ever heard it before. I can't see outside. I covered all the windows to stop any light escaping out to the street.

Where are the cats, the dogs, the foxes? Did the zombies kill them? Did only the birds survive because they could fly to safety?

The birdsong is a good sign. I think it shows the infection can't cross species. Or, at least, not to birds. I'm probably reading too much into it. I mean, what do I know about how infections spread? If bird flu can mutate to humans, then why not the other way around? Perhaps it's just a matter of time. Perhaps I should just enjoy the sound of there being something else alive

13:00

It's definitely not my reduced mobility. Nor is it boredom or even loneliness. No, it's that I've become more systematic in my looting methodology. More experienced, if you like. More professional. That's what I told myself as I went through the house room-by-room, drawer-by-drawer. Whatever it is, it isn't nosiness. Honestly, it's not.

Okay, who am I trying to fool? I don't even believe it myself. The jury's still out on whether I'm lonely, but I'm definitely bored and confined to moving around very, very slowly. Whatever the reason, my prying has paid off. You won't guess what I found. No, you have to guess. Go on, try. Three guesses. Give up? See, I knew you wouldn't get it.

Easter eggs. Small ones, but bona fide, honest to goodness, thirty-percent cocoa, milk chocolate Easter eggs. They're the kind they marketed to kids. Small, hollow eggs in big cardboard boxes with mazes on the back and the tips on how to organise your own Easter egg hunt. I found six of them. And, before you ask, no, they weren't hidden. They were in a carrier bag in a dresser in the front room.

Chocolate. Say it again. Chocolate. Oh, is there anything so wonderful? I've only had a very small piece, I don't know how good chocolate is on an empty and seriously upset stomach, but I just had to taste it. How long has it been since I had any? A month? Maybe longer, I can't remember. I couldn't even remember how it tasted.

I wonder who bought them, whether it was John or May. I know it's John and May, that's what their friends called them. The gas and electric people knew them as James and Mai Embery. I like how they had two sets of names, one for people they knew and one for those they didn't. It's like a code, a secret password to their own private club. I've always approved of nicknames, people without them struck me as less honest somehow. I wonder which one of them planned that far ahead? I know the supermarkets used to put the Easter displays out around Boxing Day, but I didn't think anyone actually bought them that early.

Or maybe it was Chuck, whose teachers called him Ronald. His real name, at least the name on his NHS card, is Charleston. That must be some kind of family name so Chuck makes sense, but the Ronald thing? His English teacher apparently decided to call him Ronald on account of 'Chuck' not being appropriate for the school. Going by the letter of complaint May wrote, that teacher was a textbook underachiever with a serious chip on his shoulder. Seriously, what kind of school in this day and age employs a teacher like that? Poor kid, he's only ten. Maybe those were his Easter eggs. Maybe he planned ahead, and bought them with his Christmas money the moment they went on sale.

No, on second thought that doesn't seem like him, not going by the mess in his room. When he was packing, he must have emptied every drawer and cupboard. After he'd either found everything he wanted or, more likely, filled his meagre bag allowance, he tried stuffing things back in. May must have been furious with the mess. Or maybe it was John who did the housework.

They couldn't take much with them, only what they could fit in the car. They must have been planning a long trip before the outbreak, because they had some petrol. They headed out by car, but they weren't intending to drive the whole way. On the roof, or maybe strapped to the back, they had their bikes.

In the garage, next to a workbench, is a photo of the family, all five of them, all bedecked in seriously hard-core cycling gear. Well, all save the daughter. She's wearing strategically ripped jeans and far too much make-up for a cycling holiday. It's quite funny really. She must have spent hours working on 'a look'. What she didn't consider was that a few hours cycling up a mountain in the wind and rain would turn her into a throwback to the eighties. I don't think I've ever seen hair quite that big. She does *not* look happy. Everyone else does, though, and not entirely at her expense.

I'm not sure where the photo was taken. Judging by Chuck's height, it can't have been more than a year or two ago. Maybe that was their first proper cycling tour together as a family. I bet that was the year that Chuck had his first new proper bike and he was finally old enough to go along with them.

It's nice.

There's no car in the garage, no car outside either. Five bikes are missing from the rack in the garage. There are some spare saddles and tyres, all thin ones designed for speed, but none of the thicker cross-country ones. They must have taken those with them.

I don't know where they've gone, not exactly. They didn't leave a note. Why would they? Well, if they were expecting either of their kids to come here looking for them, they would. Which means they've either gone to Exeter, where their son's a second-year undergrad, or Dundee where their daughter's in her fourth year. It's term time, and I'm assuming that's where they are, based on the copies of the course schedules pinned to the kitchen notice board.

The plan must be to meet up with their son first. Exeter's about a hundred and sixty miles from here. Would they have enough petrol to get there? Probably, but that would run the tank dry. Certainly, there's no way they could have found more once they'd left, not with the rationing. So after Exeter, they'd be on their bikes. The numbers don't add up though, four of them, but five bikes. Maybe Douglas, that's the son's name, has a friend. Or perhaps John and May are planning on picking someone up along their way. They've taken an extra bike, that's the important point. It's for someone else, I'm sure. They're going out of their way to help someone else. I like that about them. The Emberys. Nice people.

I don't care what you say. What I say is that they cycled up mountain, through valley, and across dale, all the way to Scotland. They collected Simone, and then they headed off into the highlands where, right now, they're happily eating porridge and shortbread. They'll survive this, the five of them and whomever that extra bike was for. They'll thrive up there, safe, secure, until one day they decide to come back.

17:00

Dinner time, and it's da, da, da, daa! More pasta. This time, for a change of pace, I'm having the ones shaped like seashells. Same as breakfast, same as dinner last night, and the same as dinner tomorrow and the next, roughly, eleven days after that. These guys seriously liked the stuff. I'm guessing that this isn't the ordinary shop stuff, not the stuff I'd buy anyway. It must have been organic, or handmade by Italian grannies in some remote hillside village. Why else would they have put it on display in the middle of the kitchen-island? Today's special has been cooked in orange juice, and it isn't bad. At least, it's no worse than anything else I've had lately.

Which brings me to the birds. "Four and Twenty blackbirds, baked in a pie…" People did eat them, then, long ago. I'm not there yet, but soon I'll have to stop scavenging from the remains of the old world and learn anew the skills of an even older one. But not yet. It's one more step on the road leading away from civilisation, a step I'm not quite ready to take.

But I did take another. The dustbin in which they were storing the inner tubes has now been reassigned and is doing duty as a water-butt. Now I've got to hope it rains.

19:00

I found Lenham Hill on the map. I knew I recognised the name. It was an old Cold War broadcasting substation. It wasn't one that had ever been used, but was part of a chain of relay stations in case London was destroyed in a nuclear attack. All of those were mothballed in the early seventies when it became apparent that nowhere in the UK would survive

World War Three. The equipment had been removed long ago, though this was never made public. It was Jen's father who'd told me about this. He'd been the cabinet minister responsible.

I'm certain I've seen the name more recently than that, though. It doesn't matter. Wherever Radio Free England was transmitting from, it wasn't Lenham Hill. Whatever the purpose in those broadcasts, it wasn't what they claimed it to be.

Day 60, Woolwich, London

07:15

Rice cooked in orange juice works well. Rice Krispies with orange juice doesn't.

I found a hatchet in a box in the garage and a mountaineering axe in a box in John and May's bedroom. It looks deadly.

During the night, I had second thoughts during about the guttering. I've no idea what state it's in. Come to that, I've no idea what's in the rainwater, but I can't do much about that. I've tied one end of a groundsheet to the washing line, the other end to a camping pole, and trailed it so that any rain that falls on it will be funnelled into the bin.

Now I just need the rain. There was none last night, and not a cloud in the sky this morning.

The high fences make the garden reasonably secluded. I've checked the houses to either side and they're both empty. As long as I'm quiet, I can sit outside and watch the birds. There are far more than I ever remember seeing before, flocks of twenty or thirty of them. This must be the result of fewer predators for the hatchlings and no humans accidentally destroying their nests.

They treat the zombies the same way they used to treat cats, dogs, and any other predator, humans included. They just fly up and away to some safe roost.

I remember reading about passenger pigeons and how, before they were wiped out at the beginning of the twentieth century, their flocks could be hundreds of miles wide and billions of birds deep. I'm not saying I'm expecting that next year, but just imagine what a sight it would be.

Fish, too, they'll do well out of this. Not sure that will help me much. Can I trust the fish in the rivers? I have no idea, but I've no idea how to fish, so it's all academic.

Chickens? No, they'll all be dead from dehydration by now, the ones that weren't eaten by hungry refugees. Goats, though, there's no reason they couldn't have survived this, but where are there goat farms? There have to be *some*. After all, where there's British goat's cheese there has to be British goats. But where? I vaguely remember that the type I preferred came from Wales, but there surely has to be some nearer than that.

It's just another dream, isn't it? I picture myself searching for a goat farm, and the next image my brain throws up is of a joint roasting merrily on a spit. What about the steps in between? There are the difficult ones like catching and butchering the animals. Then there's the nearly impossible task of getting from here to a remote farm in Wales, Somerset, or Lancashire. And that can't be done until I've completed the simplest step of finding the address of a goat farm. No, in my mind those steps are just trivial irritations that can, easily, be solved. A few months ago, they would have been. I'd only have had to go online, search for a map, and then for a video titled 'Ten Easy Steps to Slaughtering a Goat'. I bet there was one.

08:30

Whenever I get maudlin, I find looting is the best tonic. If I'm to stay here much longer, I'll need more food, but four of Them have turned up in the night. They're not quite outside the house, but scattered across the street, a few houses down. I could go out the back, breaking through the fences again, but that might attract Them. I'll just sit, wait, and read.

15:00

Just finished *Great Expectations*. *David Copperfield* next. Still no rain.

19:00

I've been sitting up in Chuck's bedroom, staring through his skylight at the clouds as the sun set. It's a great view. He's got glow in the dark stars and planets on his ceiling, posters of the solar system on the walls, and a telescope in the corner. No prizes for guessing what he wanted to be when he grows up.

I doubt he'll have the chance. If he makes it, he'll fish or be a farmer. We all will. I don't mind the idea of being a farmer. It'd be good to eat the food I've grown from scratch. Not that I have a clue how to do it, but there are books, right? I know we closed all the libraries, but I'm sure some zealous kitchen gardener somewhere will have a book or two I can loot.

Day 61, Woolwich, London

09:00

In the final days before the evacuation, the removal of the PM caused only one major problem. A fleet of boats was heading across the Atlantic towards Britain. A flotilla is a better word for it, since there was no real coordination between the craft, made up of fishing boats, pleasure cruisers, launches, cigarette boats, and even some rafts. They were refugees from across the Americas, just ordinary people looking for somewhere safe. Some had been at sea for days. Others had turned back from Greenland, where a similar fleet was swamping what had looked like the most promising redoubt on the planet.

We tried to communicate with them, to tell them to turn back, but there was no one in charge, no one to cajole or threaten. The only bribe we could offer was the one thing they wanted and the one thing we were not prepared to give: sanctuary.

The captain of one of the fishing boats, Sophia Augusto, tried to reason with us via a tenuous link relayed through a coastguard vessel. She'd set off with her extended family from Puerto Rico, three days after New York, about the same time as I was being driven home from hospital. Initially, she'd thought that it would be safer at sea, that the infection would burn itself out and that order would be restored. As the days went by, it became clear that the world they'd known had disappeared forever. She tried to persuade us that there were no zombies in the flotilla. That they'd all been at sea for days, and none of the vessels were large enough to hide one of the undead, but that just wasn't good enough for us. She was told that there would be a place for her and any other trawlers, but not for the rest, and that wasn't good enough for her.

Our naval resources were stretched thin. Though we had some vessels in the Atlantic, most of our fleet was deployed to tackle refugees coming from Europe. All that was readily available, all that we had to destroy a fleet of thousands, was a Trident submarine. It was ordered to fire off a nuclear missile, and to detonate it above this flotilla. The captain refused. The orders, after all, were coming from the foreign secretary, not the PM.

I'm not sure what happened to that submarine. Jen wouldn't tell me, and by then, though Sholto was still sending information through, I was getting few replies to any messages I sent him.

I don't know what happened to that flotilla either. Some of our conventional naval assets were retasked, but I don't know if they reached the ships or if, when they did, they fired any shots.

Perhaps that is how the infection came to our island in numbers greater than those we could manage. Perhaps not. I listened to the recording, and there was something in Sophia Augusto's voice that made me believe and trust her over that of the admiral with whom she was pleading.

17:00

Still no rain.

How long will the Thames Barrier hold? Not forever. One day something will just go wrong, some piece of the mechanism will fail, and London, or at least this part of it, will flood. I can't stay here, but if I'm going to escape, it won't be on foot, so I spent the day looking for a bicycle.

158

When I checked outside this morning, the zombies in the street had moved to the junction. There's five of them now, squatting there, torpid, unmoving. Sentinels, that's the best way to describe Them, silent sentinels.

I broke off part of the fence on the side of the garden furthest from those sentinels, and made my way through the neighbouring garden. Then it was through another fence at the back of that property. I kept on breaking through fences and crawling across overgrown lawns until I found a deserted stretch of road. It took a long time, since I had to work and move quietly. I couldn't risk using a saw. Instead, I pulled out the nails, one at time.

I'm becoming adept at spotting the houses where the living dead are still inside. It's the simple, subtle signs. Like the glass littering the patio where a window has been broken from the inside, or the way birds will hesitate before landing on the roof. Or it's the discarded tools and spilled blood showing where a fight had begun outside, and the scratches on the open doors betraying that it had ended inside. In some, those with a closed door, I peered through the window but saw shadows that don't appear quite right. I stuck to the back gardens, wandering the neighbourhood, my route decided by the houses the undead were in and the streets They were on.

I spotted a bike after a few hours. It was leaning against a garage wall in a house a few streets from the Emberys'. I couldn't see the zombie, but I knew one was somewhere in the garden. Through a knothole in the neighbouring house's fence I saw that the lawn had been recently trampled, but the windows to the house were neither boarded up nor covered.

Using an out-sized plant-pot as a mounting block, I pulled myself up a pear tree, its fruit still a few months away from being ripe. I shimmied across a branch until I was higher than the fence, made sure I had the mountaineering axe ready in my hand, its loop tied securely around my wrist, then jumped across and down.

As the zombie moved slowly from a gap between the conservatory and the side wall, I moved the crutch forward, ready to take my weight. As the creature drew closer, its dead eyes flecked with those same strands of grey

I've now seen countless times, it seemed as if all became still. The flapping of a loose sole from one of its trainers was the only sound I could hear. Then it raised its arms, far thinner than those of the living, and the action brought air wheezing into its lungs. Its hands, the skin shrunken and shrivelled, grasped towards me. I brought the axe down. It went straight through the skull and stuck there. I tried to get it out, but I'd have needed to split the thing's head right open to do it.

The bike was leaning against the wall as if someone, perhaps the one I'd just killed, had been about to ride it. How terrible that must have been, to have been ready to leave, only to have been infected in that moment before escape. I briefly searched the house, but found nothing. The place had that turned-over air of neglect that comes from someone living in it until long after there was any reason left to stay. I did find some photos, and they might have been of the zombie I killed, but with its skin peeling away I can't be certain.

Inside the garage was one of the oddest sights I've seen. Row upon row of empty bottles lining the shelves. Two hundred and thirteen plastic water bottles of various makes, surely too many for the collection to have started since the outbreak. Maybe not, that's just another story that's never going to get told.

All that had been of any value in this new world had been packed into a bag on the bike. An overflowing gutter and a month or more of exposure to the elements had turned both the bag and its contents into nothing more than a rotten mess.

I left the bicycle in the garden of a house on the other side of the block. Getting it over the fences proved too noisy and I woke up three of the undead. They didn't spot me, but heard the noise and followed me to this street. They are now lurking a few houses down.

Day 62, Woolwich, London

Another surge has begun. I think that's a better term for it. Whenever I think of hordes I'm reminded of Genghis Khan and nomadic horsemen sweeping down from the steppe. With that image comes the implied coordination and forethought that's as misleading as the insectile notions of swarms and plagues. They are a storm raging upon the Earth that one day will cease, leaving nothing but a ravaged, twisted landscape speckled with their own bleached bones.

Still no rain.

Day 63, Woolwich, London

I've taken to sitting up in the attic, watching as They go by. Dozens pass each hour, all heading east, as if They are following a course parallel to the river. Where they go and whence they came… How does that line end?

Are They like waves in the sea? Or ripples in a pond. Or, like a butterfly flapping its wings and causing a storm a thousand miles away, is some small involuntary jerk of one copied and replicated by all those nearby, then replicated again and again until the whole dead country spasms into purposeless motion? From space, does it look like a storm cloud, moving slowly across the landscape heading first towards one coast and then back towards another? Is it the same on the continent, just on a much larger scale?

And where are They going?

Day 64, Woolwich, London

13:00

Still no rain. The clouds looked promising this morning, dark and tempestuous. But they rolled by, offering nothing but a solitary rumbling salute as they sailed overhead.

17:00

Rain. Finally! I'm not sure how much, inches at least, but how much will I collect?

19:00

It's still raining. I've been taking the saucepans and jugs, the kettle, basins, and bowls, and anything else I can find outside, filling up every inch of lawn. If this keeps up…

If only this keeps up…

Day 65, Woolwich, London

15:00

The rain stopped at some point before dawn. I've got about ten litres of water. I thought there would be more. It's not bad, but not enough to waste on washing, just enough to survive for a few more days.

I've retrieved the bike. It took most of the day. It would probably have been easier to have taken all my gear there, but this house has begun to feel like home. More of a home than that flat was, anyway.

18:00

A bit more rain this afternoon. I managed to collect another litre. After boiling the water and washing my leg, I've about nine litres left. I know I said I wasn't going to waste any on washing, but the leg is different. The metal in the brace keeps rubbing at the skin. I need to keep the wounds clean and the straps sterile. I can't risk an infection. Ha! I can't use that word, can I? I'll need to come up with something else to describe my fear of gangrene, sepsis, and any other of a million life-threatening complaints that now seem benign by comparison.

I've decanted my boiled rainwater into bottles I'd lined up on the coffee table before I remembered what I had seen in that garage. Whatever madness caused someone to collect and display those bottles is not something I wish to reproduce. Nine litres left. I can survive like this, scavenging food, not washing, hiding, scared of the dark. Yes, I can survive like this, but surviving isn't the same as living. I want to have a bath. I want to feel clean again. I want to stop spending every spare minute worrying about food and water.

That's what I'll have to look for, somewhere with water, perhaps by a river. Perhaps a cottage with a stream running through the back, with a chicken coop shaded by fruit trees, and perhaps a cow or two grazing on the front lawn. I'll fish in the summer, live on eggs in the winter, roast one of the older chickens on Christmas Day. At Easter, I'll paint six eggs in memory of the ones I found in this house. I'll find a book on beekeeping in the library, perhaps even travel back to London to raid Kew for pineapples or bananas.

Except I won't. Not as long as They still plague the land.

There's a strange smell in the air. It's one of decay, but not of death. The city is beginning to rot as walls remain unpainted, and brick begins to crack, as trees and bushes take root in walls, and storm drains block and overflow. It is the necrotic odour of our civilisation's end.

Day 66, Woolwich, London

05:30

I re-read my entries to date last night. Far too gloomy. Far too introspective and a good deal too poetic. I blame an excess of Dickens, and too much conversation with myself. As a result, I have determined to talk to myself less, and be more proactive.

Hindsight is a stalwart of politics, of course, and something I've relied upon and detested in equal measure, but while there are countless courses of action I could have taken, and many different routes I could have travelled, here I am.

Maybe I can't have a cottage by a stream, but there's no reason I can't have something just as good. A stream *could* work. I could *make* it work, if I followed it up-river to its source to make sure it was clear and clean, but why not just go to the source? What I need is a well. I know of none in south London, or anywhere else for that matter. Perhaps there's a London mineral water company I've not heard of. Perhaps there were even walking tours of London's working wells that every school kid goes on. Like learning to name the stars, fly a plane, or fire a gun, it's one of those things I've just never done.

The Emberys have maps, lots of maps, bought, I assume for their cycling tours of the world. The few that are of the UK are large road maps, showing the motorways and major roads, but none with enough detail as to include any wells. I could search the neighbouring houses, and perhaps I'd get lucky, finding some old tourist brochure at the bottom of a drawer, but it seems unlikely.

What I'm looking for is a community that was established long before the infection, one that eschews the modern conveniences of piped water, electric heat, and gas cooking. One that was self-sufficient, with crops already planted. To that end I need to find God, or, rather, a monastery.

There. Now I have a goal. I also have a starting point, so how do I get from one to the other? I don't think the Emberys were religious. There are no priests or vicars listed in their address book. No imams, rabbis, or gurus either, but, speaking of some recent tragedy, there was the address of a funeral home. It's only three roads and a handful of side streets from here, maybe a kilometre, maybe a mile, and it's in the same direction as the house where I found the bike.

The funeral home should lead me to a church, the church to a monastery, the monastery to water.

But if I'm going out again, then I first need a better weapon. I have an idea for one.

164

12:30

Weapon, version one, is ready. In a dim light it looks like a cross between a scythe and a pike. I've used the extendible tree shears I found in the garage as a frame. That's a metal tube in three two-metre-long segments that has a pair of jaws with a blade at one end, a handle at the other and a wire running down the inside. I had one back at the house. They were unwieldy as hell, and exhausting to use, but at a cost of a hundred pounds, it was far cheaper than getting a gardener in every year to trim the fir trees in the front garden. That gave me the height. I'm using a shelving bracket padded with part of a saddle as a handle to go under my arm, with more padding further up if I want to use it as a staff. At the end, I've strapped on the blade from the garden shears.

It won't be very durable, since it's all held together with cord, brake cables and tape, but give me a break here; it's my first time having a go at this. I've practised in the garden and it's sturdy enough as a walking stick. Whether it'll work as a weapon, I'll find out soon.

19:10

Today, for the first time, I went out looking for one of Them. I wanted to test my pike and wanted to do it on my terms. It was very different to be the hunter for once, and not the hunted. And I learned a lot from the experience. Firstly, I learned that, after I break into a property and clear it, I need a way of securing the doors. When I got back this evening, the front door to the house was ajar. When I left, I just pulled it shut and some errant breeze must have blown it open. It took a nerve-wracking hour to check each room, and another to double-check, before I felt safe once more.

But back to my experiment with the pike. I crawled through the back gardens until I reached my test-house. I'd spotted the glass littering the ground from where an upstairs window had been smashed from the inside. As quietly as I could, I broke in.

As I went through the house checking each room, I kept one ear on what was going on inside and the other on what was going on outside. It wasn't easy to concentrate on both, and to be honest, the whole experience was utterly terrifying. My second lesson was to do any future tests out in the open.

As for the pike itself, it's far too unwieldy for inside work. I'd thought that experimenting with it inside would be safer. As long as I had my back to the door, I'd have somewhere to retreat to, and with the fenced-in gardens I needn't fear being surrounded. What I'd not considered was how much extra noise I'd make as the pike clattered against the walls and ceiling. Perhaps because of that, it should have been no surprise that the zombie heard me before I found it. As I retreated to the back door, it lumbered down the stairs. When the zombie tried to grab me through the banisters, it stumbled, tripping on its dressing gown's cord, and fell down the remaining stairs. I dropped the pike, snatched the hatchet from my belt, stepped forward, and split its skull while it was still trying to get back to its feet.

That's only the third time I've seen a zombie in night attire. I find the notion that anyone, on being infected, would take the time to change before lying down in bed unsettling.

I picked up the pike and went outside. As the adrenaline faded, I could feel the fear building. I wanted to give up. I wanted to go back to the Emberys' house and not come out again. Instead, I headed through the gardens, then across the road towards the house where I'd found the bicycle.

My second target was hibernating in the middle of a curved stretch of road. I checked that there were no other zombies around, and stepped out into the street. It spotted me from about twenty metres away. Or perhaps it heard me, because I'm now sure that is the sense which They use the most. The zombie took its time getting to its feet, barely finishing its second step before my blow came down, right on its crown. Its head split open, but the blade came loose, and almost came off, as I pulled it free from the dead creature's skull.

I've made some adjustments, affixed a heavier counterweight, and reattached the blade. Tomorrow I'm off to the funeral home.

Day 67, Shooters Hill, London

15:00

It's an oddly disquieting experience being surrounded by coffins inside while the undead are outside. It's made worse when one is, well, I'd not say trapped, I've been trapped before and this is nothing like that. I'm just detained here a little longer than I'd like.

The funeral home is at the southern end of Plumstead, near Shooters Hill. It's a 1950s building at the end of a terrace of shops, most of which were boarded up long before the outbreak. The staff car park and entrance are at the back. The customer entrance is at the front, and that leads into a small, bleak waiting room and a, frankly, tasteless showroom. Not customer, sorry, the bereaved. The basement is, I assume, where they prepare the bodies. Maybe it's not, but access is through a very sturdy, very closed door. There's no sound coming from down there, and I'm not surprised. Even so, there's no way I'm going to unlock that door.

I took my time coming here. Not that, these days, there's any way of travelling except cautiously. I'd hoped to find a route with empty streets, but no such luck. Despite my best efforts, I had no choice but to deal with two zombies. I killed both with swings to the head, but the pike held up well. On balance, yes, I think it's a weapon that will work.

I entered the funeral home through the back door, so I didn't see the pack in the street at the front of the building. Pack, yes, that's about right. I didn't notice the pack until after I'd found the address book. It was in the drawer of the desk in the upstairs office. By the state of the small break room, someone had already scavenged here. Everything edible had gone, no tea, no coffee, no biscuits, no sugar, nothing. The cupboards were open, even the cutlery had been removed from the drawers. Whoever was here before me made a far more thorough search of the place than I usually do.

As I went back through the office, looking at it now with the eye of a looter, I thought to check the small cupboard under the desk. It was, I thought, the right sort of spot for the senior funeral director to keep his secret stash. No such luck. If there was anything ever there, it's long gone. It was while I was standing there that I happened to look out the window.

The undead aren't outside the funeral home, though there are a few idling within a few metres of the front door. There's another forty or so between here and the main pack, and that's about a hundred strong. They're gathered around a large office building at the other end of the street.

Across two of the windows at the front is a banner with one word, 'Help'.

16:00

The address book lists churches but not by denomination. Is there a way to tell just by the name? I mean do Anglican churches use some saints, Catholics the others? The depth of my ignorance surprises me sometimes. There are two relatively close to one another, about a mile south of the Emberys' home. Since I doubt there'd be two of the same flavour adjacent to each other, that's a good place to look.

That just leaves the question of the building up the street. Are there still any survivors there? By now they could easily have run out of food and water. Perhaps they decided not to wait until that happened and have already left. No. The waves of zombies travelling through the city would have dragged the undead outside the building with Them. This pack must have gathered there in the last few days. It could be that the undead are drawn to that building not by a human sound, but by something automatic, but surely even batteries would have run out by now. But what can I do about it?

All I can think of is getting Them to chase me. If I'm going to risk that then I need to categorically know that there is someone alive inside there. I've brought two days' worth of supplies with me. If there's no sign of life by mid-morning tomorrow then I'll head back.

I've broken the mirror that was hanging in the toilet, and will use a shard of that to try to signal. Here goes.

19:00

Ah, great. Superb. There are people in there.

The flashing mirror got no response. I figured I'd take it a step further and since it was getting dark, tried flashing my torch on off, on off, on off, pause. On off , on off, pause. On off, pause and so on. I have a response. Someone is alive inside there and what's more, they know Morse code. For the second time in as many months, I wish that I did. I repeated their sequence back at them, hoping they'd understand I didn't know what they were saying.

So, what do I do now?

20:30.

No further response. I need to come up with a plan to help them escape.

Day 68, Shooters Hill, London

05:00

I can't think of a way to communicate with the survivors in that building without the undead knowing I'm here. But I can't just leave them be. Not if I want to keep my membership of the human race. Not after Sam. Not after thinking I was truly alone.

17:00, Woolwich, London

I'm back at the Emberys' house. I'm safe. Whoever those survivors are, wherever they are, they've escaped, and I helped.

My first idea was to try one of the cars, to set off the alarm, or rig a horn to go off. Of the three I tried, the batteries were flat. In the end I went back to the funeral home, threw a chair out of the window, and then started hurling down the computer, the paperweights, and anything else I could grab until I was sure that the pack was heading towards me. Then I ran, but I didn't run far.

I wanted to know that the zombies had moved from the office building to gather around the funeral home, but I also wanted to make sure They weren't following me. The last thing I wanted was to end up under siege at the Emberys'. When I was sure that They hadn't followed, I started retracing my steps. I was about two hundred yards away when I heard shouting, about a hundred and fifty yards away when I heard an engine start.

By the time I was close enough to see the street, the vehicle had gone. So had whoever was inside, leaving behind nothing but a few corpses and a dozen twitching bodies that had been run over in the escape.

Maybe they left details of where they were going in that building. I'm not going to check. The undead that had trapped them were heading east, following the sound of that vehicle. Now, too many zombies lie between me and wherever they've gone.

Day 69, Woolwich, London

Last night, I couldn't sleep. I'm not the only survivor. I don't think I wrote it down or even said it out loud, but I thought I was the only one. I think I began to believe it.

There are other people out there. I didn't see them, but they are there. That was my first real contact with a human since Sam, and this was far more real. Those people are alive because of me. What counts, what's important, the only thing that really matters, is that if they survived, then there will be others.

I feel like Robinson Crusoe, knowing that King and Empire is out there. Somewhere, across the impossibly wide ocean, as distant as the stars, yet indisputably still there. Yesterday was like seeing the masts of a ship against the horizon. Impossibly distant, and in no way a rescue, but evidence that there is a wider world still out there, that life can go on and that one day rescue may come.

Who wrote Robinson Crusoe? I thought it was Stevenson, but he wrote *Treasure Island*, didn't he? Was it Dumas, or did he write *The Count of Monte Cristo*? I can't remember. Maybe it wasn't Stevenson. Maybe it wasn't King and Empire. That's one more book I must find.

Day 70, Woolwich, London

Before the outbreak, bikes were making a real comeback in the UK. We had the state-sponsored ones, of course, the designated train carriages, the cycle lanes, and the recumbents. But my absolute favourite were the parents with the cargo bikes, driving their children around like miniature rickshaw cabs.

The Emberys' children were far too old for that, but they do have panniers. One, I think, was designed to carry a suit, but it fits on the bike and I'm asking for nothing more. The tyres are pumped up, the brakes work, and the bags are full. Water, food, a change of socks. A few tools, some washing line in lieu of rope, the A-Z, the flashlight, and spare batteries. A D-lock in lieu of any chain for securing the doors to wherever I choose to lay my head, the last of the vitamin tablets, aspirin, and paracetamol. I've got the address book from the funeral home, and since I've carried them this far, the laptop and the hard drive. What am I missing? It's a heavy enough load as it is.

I've checked and double-checked, and don't think I'm leaving anything behind that I'll regret.

15:30

A spare tyre! I can probably get a few miles on a flat one, but if I do get a flat in the middle of nowhere, I don't fancy walking. I've strapped two to the back of the bike, they're all the thin, narrow racing type, but that's better than nothing. I suppose if I find thicker tyres, I'll need thicker wheels, too. What about gears and the chain, will I need to replace those as well? Perhaps it would be easier to look for a whole new bike. No. I'm ready to go, no more stalling.

16:00

I forgot the wok. That's now tied on. I can't guarantee finding an open fireplace the next time I fancy a cuppa. Add in spare matches, the grill tray, and the second smallest saucepan, and I'm worried I've packed too much. I've added some spare brake cables to the packs as well. I don't have any idea how you attach them, but better to have them and try than miss them and end up on foot.

I've got four litres of water. Enough, I think, for four days. I'm leaving the rest of the food, all sealed in plastic boxes, and a note on the door. It's quite a large one that reads 'SAFE!' Maybe if I get back here I'll find others at home. If. But I don't think I'll be coming back.

I'll head to the church, and from there to a monastery. If I can't find an address book, or if the churches are inaccessible, then I'll just keep going until I'm as far away from London as I can get.

Day 71, Woolwich, London

05:30

Off we go.

12:15, near Croydon, London

It feels so good to be outside!

They say you never forget how to ride a bike. It would be better to say you never forget how to fall off a bike. Three wheels would be better. I'd be able to charge at Them like a knight of old. As it is, I've almost fallen off trying to avoid Them. But the bike is fast, zombies are slow, and most importantly, They don't hear me coming.

I've stopped a couple of times this morning, whenever I think it's safe, just to see if I am being followed. There have been a few trailing behind me, but not many. I really think this is going to work.

There was a zombie at the end of the road near the house. It was lanky creature, wearing a tattered trench coat ripped almost in two along the back. I thought I could pass it before it noticed me. I would have, except that there were another two that I didn't see until it was almost too late. They were crouched down behind a ragged hedge. I saw them just as they began to rise. I swerved, lost my footing, and almost fell off. They were on their feet, moving towards me, summoning others with that wheezing rasp of theirs.

I was barely above walking speed when I reached the zombie in the trench coat. It grabbed at me, missing my arm by inches. Its hand tangled in the bag I'd hung from the handlebars. With my good leg on the ground, I kicked it squarely in the chest with my bad leg. The weight of the brace added the extra heft needed to knock it to the ground, my bag still in its grip.

That's the A-Z, a bottle of water, and a day's worth of food gone. I'll find another map somewhere around here, then get an idea of where I am. Without the map, I got lost in the side streets, and couldn't find the churches I was looking for. That's no real setback, I've seen a dozen today, none where I felt I could stop, but I'll find one sooner or later.

I'm still in London, I'm not sure exactly where, but about two miles from Croydon, according to the road signs. A few streets back, I caught sight of the towering office blocks. Even without the road signs I'd have known which way to look; the largest plume of smoke in south London is coming from there. Croydon is burning down again. The two tower blocks I could see were unaffected, but it can't be long before that fire spreads and then, well, then it'd be best not to be anywhere near here.

I've managed about ten miles so far today, not quite the forty I'd hoped for but better than I've managed in all the weeks I've been travelling. I'd forgotten how many hills there are in London. I'm trying to avoid the undead as much as possible and that's adding something to the journey time, but with no specific place to go, why hurry? I've found roads blocked by trees, others by stalled cars, others crowded with the undead.

I've seen countless storm drains blocked, overflowing gutters, broken windows, and an abundance of wallflowers taking root in the Victorian red brick. I've seen birds, squirrels, and even, I think, a cat, but no humans. No survivors. All I can see is desolation. All I can smell is decay. All I can hear is the creaking, cracking sigh of undead voices on the wind, yet all I feel is hope.

18:00, near Reigate, Surrey

I'm at a garden centre, though after months of inattention, most of the plants have died. A few potted trees and bushes in the area open to the sky have survived. Shoots are peeking through some of the cracks in the concrete. Even so, it's a pretty grim place. Someone has been here before me. Most of the sharper and heavier tools are gone. The break room and vending machine have been cleared of anything edible or drinkable. I did find a selection of water-butts outside. They were part of a display on water conservation. Wonderfully, and thanks to the rain, they were full.

The rear of the garden centre backs onto a railway line. The embankment is pretty steep. Too steep for the undead to climb, I think. I hope. Certainly, it's too steep for me to climb without using my hands. Since They don't have that level of coordination, I don't need to worry about any of Them coming from that direction while I sleep.

I *did* find a church, and got a directory that lists all the institutions in the south of England. It's a handwritten address book that doesn't differentiate between churches and monasteries. I suppose I shouldn't expect to find a book titled 'In the event of the apocalypse, head here'. Not in a church, anyway.

The old and heavy stone, thick oak doors, and tall windows above a grasping arm's reach, would have made it a good place to hide out for a few days. Possibly longer. Behind the church was a house with a secluded garden, complete with fruit trees and high walls. Land to grow, walls to keep me safe. It was almost perfect. Almost. The pews weren't empty.

There was no sign of struggle or violence, just row upon row of bodies. I guess they'd taken some kind of poison, but who knows? From the level of decomposition, they died soon after the outbreak. I don't know if this was the original congregation or some group that had banded together after the evacuation. I didn't see any point trying to find out.

I closed the doors and left them there. I don't resent them, nor do I pity their final hours. It was their choice and it's not for me to judge, but I think that priest in Colombia had the right of it, that what we should fear most in this terrible world is fear itself.

I've had to tighten the leg brace. The constant pedalling, even at my sedate pace, has loosened the straps. As for my leg, I don't think it's healed properly. Let me rephrase that, I *know* it hasn't healed properly. It aches incessantly with a dull heat that's barely dented by paracetamol, but that's all I've got. There's no point dwelling on it. The water is almost boiling. Tonight I sleep. Tomorrow I go on.

Day 72, near Alton, Surrey

18:00

I saw a signpost a few miles back. London is now forty miles away to the northeast. The town of Alton is about two miles away to the southeast. I was aiming due south, towards the coast, but about three miles from the garden centre I saw a pack of Them hovering around a lorry.

My first instinct was to turn round and get out of there, so was my second, but there had to be someone inside that lorry. Why else would the undead be gathered around it, banging and scraping at the metal? I had to do something to help. If I could.

The road travelled along a hill whose crest was to my left, at the top of a field. To my right there was another field and beyond that a cluster of houses. Beyond that was a railway and a commuter town. The lorry had swerved across the road at a junction where the road, a two-lane one, met a narrower, one-track lane.

175

Even if I ignored the occupants of the lorry there was no way that I could cycle through the undead crowding around it. There were too many to fight, and too narrow a stretch of road between the lorry and the thick hedgerow. I looked over at the town. Somewhere inside there would be food, but I could see scores of the undead, even from that distance. That only left getting to the top of the hill and following the old farm road down to wherever it led, and if I was doing that, why shouldn't I try to get the zombies to follow?

I pushed the bike up the side of the field, then along the ridge to the road from where I could look down on the junction. Both the cab and the lorry were on their sides. I couldn't see inside the cab, or discern what the cargo had been. Maybe it was food. It had to be valuable to risk travelling on such narrow roads. If there were fewer of Them around the cab, then the driver could get out through the passenger-side door. If he or she were nimble enough, they could jump onto the back of the lorry, run along its edge, and over and down into the field beyond. It was a reasonably decent escape route, as long as the driver wasn't injured. If they were, there was nothing I could do about it. I counted forty zombies, but there were bound to be on the far side of the vehicle.

I raised my arms and waved. They didn't notice me. That was frustrating. As long as I was at the top of the hill, I could get on the bike and let gravity do the rest. I didn't want to walk down towards the lorry only to have to run back up hill to escape. After a few minutes, I realised that was exactly what I had to do.

I walked forward ten paces, raised my arms, and waved. Nothing. I went another ten paces and waved again. Still nothing. I didn't want to shout. I knew that would get their attention, but it would also alert any of the undead that were on my escape route. I've learned that, as long as there are only one or two, I have no difficulty getting by Them. All I have to do is aim at one side of the road and the zombie will head towards me, then I wait until I'm within twenty feet of it before I swerve to the opposite side. On the few occasions there have been more, it's only been my monumental good luck that's kept me safe.

I was fifty paces from the top of the hill when a zombie finally spotted me. I waited as it started moving towards me. I kept waiting while a second, then a third, began their slow march up the hill. I waited until twenty of Them were approaching, then I trudged back up the hill. I didn't move fast, not even fast by my standards. I kept turning around to check They were following. By the time I reached the hill's crest, the nearest was where I'd been standing when it had spotted me. There were none left around the lorry. I waited a few seconds more, hoping I would see the cab door open, see some sign of life from inside, but there was no movement. I got on the bike, turned in the saddle, and then I waited some more.

The zombie in the lead started to move, not faster but more frenetically. It was as if it was trying to speed up, but the camber of the hill and its own dried-up muscles prevented it. I took one last look at the lorry and raised my hand in a final farewell. With the closest zombie no more than twenty paces away, I released the brake and kicked off from the ground. I didn't even have to pedal.

I was twenty metres down the road when the first zombie reached the crest of the hill. When I next glanced behind, there were a dozen following me, but I was a hundred metres ahead. By the time I got to the junction three miles down the road, the zombies were no longer in sight.

Perhaps They didn't all follow me. Perhaps, when I disappeared over the top of the hill, the zombies turned back to the poor soul in the cab of that lorry, someone who was perhaps too scared to act quickly enough to get away. But I don't think so. It's hard to tell which sounds are real and which are imagined, at least when it comes to those sounds of the old world, but I think I heard a long blast of the horn. I think the driver seized the moment and got away, and that horn's blast was their final salute, a goodbye and thank-you. I gave them a chance, and anyone who's survived this long would know when to take it.

It was about an hour later that I took my second detour. I'd wanted to stick to the wider multi-lane roads. On those, it's easier to dodge the undead, and following them would lead me to the coast in less than a day. I found most are encased in metal fencing, a remnant of when they were used as an evacuation route. Those barriers had already been broken, and I used those wide and ragged breaches when I needed to cross. No doubt there would be other gaps and breaks further along the roads through which I could escape. Even so, I didn't like the feel of those enclosed roads. Each time I crossed one, I felt as if I was passing over a deep, dark pit filled with unknown horrors that were waiting to pounce. Foolish, since I know exactly what those horrors would be. Nevertheless, I stuck to the older, winding, hedge-enclosed roads whose width had been determined long ago by the size of horse-drawn carts. There, however, there often wasn't enough space to outrun Them.

Twice, I had to stop, dismount, and dispatch zombies that blocked the road. Then I reached a point where a car had swerved and crashed head on into the hedge, leaving only a narrow two-foot-gap between its bumper and the impenetrable hedge on the other side. A gap that was filled by two zombies that were now heading towards me.

I dismounted, turned the bike to face the other way in case I needed to make a quick escape, then turned to face Them. One was smaller, maybe a teenager, the other, probably male, was much older. Their clothes were little more than rags, leaving their dried-out skin exposed to the elements. They were barely recognisable as having once been human.

I braced my leg, and scythed the pike forward. The blade cut deep into the older zombie's skull. I gave my wrist a now much-practised twist, pulled it free, and swung again, killing the other before the first body had fully collapsed. I waited, listened until I was sure there were no more, then I levered the bodies into the middle of the road. I cleaned the blade, and was about to remount the bike when I saw a flash of movement out of the corner of my eye. Instinctively, and it had to be instinct because I would never knowingly have moved so fast, I swung the butt of my pike towards it. I hit it in the chest, knocking it flying ten feet.

A rabbit!

I'd killed it, and not, I think, from a head wound. At this point, as it's roasting on the fire, I don't really care whether it's infected or not. I thought about it for a long while on my ride here, but I don't think it is. Its blood looked normal enough when I skinned it, or did my best at skinning it. I think if the birds are unaffected then so too are the animals. I'm going to make sure it's well cooked, though.

The smell of roasting meat! Not just roasting meat, but meat I killed myself. That's something I've never done before. It officially makes me a Hunter, very definitely with a capital 'H'.

I've got to get better at butchering, and I've got to find out what parts of the insides of animals you can eat, which you can't, and how to tell the difference. That's another book to find.

Not much eating on a single rabbit. Still, no complaints tonight.

After killing the rabbit, I had to take one more diversion, this time around a blocked coach. It was stuck in the middle of the road, at a steep bend. When I stopped, I was close enough to read the garage's name on the licence plate, more than close enough for the zombies in the backseat to see me.

I could probably have squeezed past the coach, but I had no idea why it had stopped there or whether the doors at the front were open. As They hammered on the window, I turned around and headed back the way I'd come.

It was inevitable. I'd been heading in a roughly southwesterly direction all day, and I'd woken the undead. They'd followed me. There were far too many to stop and deal with individually. Five times I was almost dragged off the bike before I found a road I'd not previously travelled on. Then I just pedalled and kept on pedalling until I was alone once more.

I'm thoroughly lost now, in an old barn at the edge of a field. Possibly in Surrey, possibly in Hampshire. I've rabbit for dinner, enough water that I don't need to find more tonight, and a strong door to keep me safe while I sleep. Who could ask for anything more?

Day 73, Brazely Abbey, Hampshire

I think I've found my sanctuary, Brazely Abbey.

This morning, after an hour of cycling with no greater aim than heading towards the coast, I spotted a sign for Brazely. It's a small hamlet in the Hampshire Downs consisting of five houses, a bus stop, a disused phone booth, and not much else. But I remembered the name from the address book. It took another hour to find the abbey, a secluded ruin hidden down an unpaved track, a quarter of a mile from the road.

It's not at all what I thought an abbey would look like. The old abbey had been burned down during the Reformation, but the land had been bought back. According to the information board, they've been restoring it for the past fifty years, but it has two important features: a stone wall that's survived centuries, and a well. A well! Fresh, clean water!

The ancient stone walls form two sides of a square. On the other sides are the newer buildings, a chapel, a dormitory, and a kitchen and shower room. It is the very epitome of the renouncing of worldly goods. Very medieval and almost perfect. Other than the well, there are beehives and an orchard, with most of the clear land given over to growing vegetables.

This is exactly what I've been looking for. There's food in the storeroom, enough for at least a couple of weeks. Plenty of building materials, too. Those must have been brought here after the outbreak. Someone has already blocked the windows and barricaded the gaps between the buildings. I think this is as good a place to live as I've found so far.

Now. Time to wash. Then to eat.

Day 75, Brazely Abbey, Hampshire

Yesterday was spent filling in the gaps around the wall. Now I can sleep knowing I won't wake to find the dormitory surrounded. That in itself has given me great peace of mind. It's a beautiful spot here, tranquil and quiet. Mostly quiet.

No doubt attracted by the sound of my labours, twice I've heard Them slouching through the woods, scattering leaf mould, breaking branches, disturbing the birds nesting in the trees. Twice I've dispatched Them, and then continued with my work.

What I didn't notice until yesterday evening, when it was almost too dark to see, were the tyre tracks. Someone was here, and as recently as last week. I'd assumed the building materials were part of the restoration work, but of course, the boarded-up windows are signs of work being done since the outbreak. For some reason, they left. I could say I hope they're coming back, but I don't know if I do. Who are these people? Are they the monks or locals? Will we get along? I know that sounds childish, but I really do feel like the kid at a new school. They were here first, after all.

Will they like me? Will they let me stay? Will they blame me for the evacuation? I could lie. I could burn this journal, but it's become part of me over these last few months. It's my only connection to the past and to the idea that there will be some kind of future.

The truth of it is that I can leave here and find somewhere else before they come back, or I can set to and help make this place a safe haven, a community from which a new society can be formed. I'm tired of running. This is where I stand.

Day 77, Brazely Abbey, Hampshire

Today is the 28th May, the day I originally thought the cast should have come off. It seems like such a long time ago I set that arbitrary milestone and started counting the days. At the time, the sole purpose of the adoption of such a distant goal was to provide a daily reassurance that there would be a tomorrow and a tomorrow after that. And now? It is seventy-seven days since the power went out in London. Seventy-seven days of this new era. Seventy-seven days since my life truly changed beyond what it would have been had the outbreak not occurred. I imagine

I've become a different person, but have I really?

I've spent the last few days working on the defences, and I've begun to believe those who were here so recently, who began the work on this place, won't be coming back.

As best as I can estimate, come harvest, there will be enough fruit and vegetables for at least twelve people for perhaps six months. It's a very rough estimate, but even so I've far more than I can possibly eat, and no way to store any of it.

With no freezers, no sugar to make jam, or vinegar for pickling, the food here will rot on the trees and I will starve come the winter. To that end, tomorrow, I will go out once more. I need to find a way of becoming self-sufficient and if I find others on my way, then so be it.

Day 78, Grange Farm Estate, Hampshire

I left at dawn. The clouds grew heavy by lunchtime. It started raining before dusk. It's rain like I've never seen it before. The sky ahead was clear, but I felt the pressure changing. I turned around in my saddle and saw ominous black clouds galloping towards me.

I've found refuge in 'The Grange Farm Estate'. It's a grand title for a collection of unprepossessing barns recently converted to holiday cottages. The path outside is under two inches of water. I'll be stuck here tonight and will have to wait until mid-morning before the ground dries out. If the rain stops.

Day 79, Grange Farm Estate, Hampshire

Still raining. Still almost pitch black outside, but I'm sure it's morning. I've not seen anything like this except on TV, and then only as a special effect.

It's impossible to know if the undead are out there, and that's more terrifying than the idea of a storm that seems to be going on forever.

There is no escape outside. The fields will have turned to mud and that mud will cover the roads. No more writing for a while. Must conserve the light's batteries.

Day 80, Grange Farm Estate, Hampshire

I was getting bored looking at the same walls, so I went to check the other cottages. The first was empty, much like this one. The second had two bodies in it. On the table was a note.

"The vaccine was a lie. The evacuation was a lie. I think, deep down, I knew that from the start. Where were they going to get the food to feed everyone? I know they said that it would be a tough few years, but we'd manage it. That 'The Indomitable Island Spirit' would prevail. That's what they said. It was a lie. The numbers just didn't add up. Food is energy, and it would take too much energy to move all those people. All those useless people with their suddenly antiquated skills were nothing but mouths to feed in a world of hunger.

I worked for the police. I was a sergeant, stuck in an admin job, collating and cataloguing evidence. It wasn't a bad life, now I look back on it, though I didn't think so at the time. A pension, a salary, and I didn't have to see anything that kept me up at night. No, it wasn't a bad life at all.

At about three a.m. on the 21st of February, the night after we started getting word in from the U.S., I was told to lock up the evidence room and report upstairs. I was given a set of riot gear and a lift to a big supermarket out near Balham. I was alone until five a.m. when another van turned up and two constables got out. Neither had even finished their training but they were decked out like me, just a bunch of coppers, you see. The Thin Blue Line.

Then the Army came. Three of them, armed like this was Afghanistan, acting like it, too. I don't know what they'd been told. They kept it between themselves.

We turned people away all day, told them it'd be re-opening soon, that there'd be rationing, but that they'd get their food. Just like we'd been told to say. For now they should go home, watch the TV, listen to the radio and keep calm. Keep calm, wasn't that ironic?

But it did stay calm, at least for us. Over the squaddie's radio we kept hearing about disturbances and calls for reinforcements, but we were okay. People came and grumbled, but they left. They were annoyed, certainly, but I also think they were glad that someone seemed to be in control.

It stayed calm right up until that night. That's when the crowd came. I don't know where they came from. Maybe they all had the same idea at the same time. At first I thought it might be from the housing estate near the station, but the clothes were wrong. About a hundred and fifty of them came marching into the car park, all demanding food.

I tried to talk to them, tried to reason with them, tried to get them to go home. One of them just laughed at me. Then she spoke in this loud clear voice that carried far beyond the car park. She said she knew the soldiers wouldn't fire. She said they weren't allowed to, not in England. She said that meant it was just three of us cops and a hundred and fifty of them. They were taking the food and it'd be easier if we just got out of the way. She said they wouldn't hurt us.

That's when her head exploded. I don't know which of the soldiers fired that first shot. I just dived to the ground as all three of them opened fire into the crowd. I lay there, waiting for it to stop, as this constant, endless staccato bam-bam-bam went on and on.

When it finally stopped, when I dared open my eyes, there were at least thirty bodies lying in the car park. The others had run. I could just make out the last one limping away.

I stood up. I don't know what I was going to do, whether I even knew. Not all the people lying there had stopped moving. Some were sobbing, some crying for help, some just screaming unintelligibly.

I started to walk towards the three soldiers. One of them, the one in charge though he wasn't wearing any insignia, he was on the radio. One of the others, the youngest, still had his rifle raised, moving it from side to side as if he was looking for a new target. The third was sobbing. As I walked back towards them, he dropped the rifle, pulled out his sidearm, and shot himself in the head.

That stopped me. I was still staring at his body when three lorries arrived. A squad of soldiers got out of the first, and half of them headed towards us. They spoke in low tones to our two soldiers, took their weapons from them, and escorted them back to the truck. Two of them picked up the one who'd committed suicide and took his body as well.

That's when I thought that actually it was okay, that they'd acted without orders, that they'd been arrested, and that this would go down as a horrible tragedy. I managed to hold onto that shred of sanity for another four seconds or so, until the next shot rang out.

The other half of that group, the soldiers who'd not relieved the two who'd been with us, they were walking amongst the crowd of bodies, shooting them in the head. Wounded or dead, they each got a bullet.

When it was over the one in charge walked over to the second lorry and slapped his hand on the side. Out came a dozen people. One of them, I recognised. Chester Carson, a petty thief who'd been on his way to graduating as a full-time fence before he'd been arrested. They'd not charged him, that I knew, they were trying to get him to do a deal.

I watched as he and the others, all wearing thick rubber gloves, picked up the bodies and threw them into the third lorry. When it was full, I watched it drive away. I waited until another lorry came, and I watched as they finished the job. I watched that fourth lorry drive off, then the one with the prisoners. Then I watched as the final lorry left, taking half the soldiers with them. And I stood there watching the soldiers that remained until I was relieved at eight o'clock the next morning.

We weren't allowed to go home. I got a few hours sleep in the station before being woken and told we were being armed. A few hours after that, a new order came in, we were all going to be kitted out in military camouflage. It was essential, apparently, to make it appear our numbers were greater than they were.

I'm not military. I'm a policeman. I believe in law and order, and as tatty as it's become, I still believe in justice. I'm a civilian in a democracy, not an executioner in a police state. I took the gun and I ran.

That's Elsie on the floor over there. I met her about a week after the 'evacuation'. I was hiding in a flat in Vauxhall. I knew there'd be no one there since its owner had been arrested the month before. I met Elsie in the lobby of the building. She was entering as I was about to leave. We decided to travel together. She didn't trust the government. That's why she stayed. That's what saved her life.

I knew of a garage that sold illegal agricultural diesel to lorry drivers, and I guessed right that it hadn't been requisitioned. We took what we could and headed west. I thought we'd be safer in Wales, or Scotland, if we could make it, but there were too many of the undead. They were everywhere. We looked for somewhere to hide. Eventually, we found it.

Elsie called it our castle, though it wasn't quite that. It had strong walls and we had some supplies, but we didn't have enough. Before we could go out looking for more, they came. Thousands and thousands of them. All night long they came, and then the next day and the day after that. I don't know where they came from, or why. At first I thought they'd never leave, that we'd starve to death. It took days, but eventually most had gone. There were only a handful outside and we dealt with them easily enough. We dragged their bodies out to a clearing and burnt them. It was the best funeral we could offer.

We needed more supplies. Our castle needed stronger walls. We needed more people. Wherever those thousands of zombies had gone, they'd be coming back. After all, what was there to stop them?

We gathered what we could from the nearby farms, killing the zombies we found nearby. We reinforced the doors and the windows. We thought we'd be safe for a month. I didn't think that was long enough.

It was my idea to go out further, to see if we could find something more. One big haul, I suppose. Something that would keep us safe for months. The car was on its last legs, but we had one fuel can left. That and what was left in the tank gave us enough for a fifty-mile round trip.

I figured, we both did, that there had to have been a plan to feed the evacuees. They'd have been expecting millions of them. That's millions of rations sitting there, waiting to be claimed. When they gave up on the evacuation, they might have taken the unused ones with them, but maybe they were in a hurry, maybe they didn't have time. It was the kind of stash we needed to last us until their bodies finally gave out and they died.

It was worth checking, but we didn't put all our eggs in one basket. We checked houses and shops. We took what we needed. We looked for signs of other people. We tried to find a way to do more than just survive.

We didn't make it to the evacuation site, but we did find another car. There were two boxes of RAF MRE rations and one box of vaccines in the boot. The box was clearly marked in stencil, 'Two Hundred, Single Use, Vaccine, Do Not Refrigerate'. No maker's label, no warnings, no side effects, just a diagram of how to inject it. I don't know what happened to the original driver, but we decided to bring both cars back to our castle. I took ours. Elsie took the one we'd just found.

By dusk, we'd reached here and decided to stop for the night, and do the final few miles in the morning.

I don't know when she took the vaccine, but she started feeling unwell around dawn. Nothing too severe to start with, just nausea and muscle cramps. At first I thought she might be pregnant. I was actually happy for this glorious half hour, until it got worse. Then I thought maybe it was something she ate, except we'd eaten exactly the same things, we'd drunk the same water. The only difference is that she took the vaccine. She'd taken it when I'd had to go outside to deal with the strays who'd followed the engine noise back here. She was scared, she said, that's why she'd taken it.

She asked me to carry her outside so she could see the sun. I knew she was dying. She couldn't even hold down any water, her skin was almost translucent and hot, so hot.

I wrapped her in a sheet and lifted her up, but she was dead before I'd reached the door. I took her outside anyway. It was her last wish, after all.

It came from behind me, biting my shoulder as we sat there together staring at the sun. I used my last bullet to kill it. Now I've brought her back inside.

Consider this a test. An experiment. I've no bullets left, and don't think I've the stomach for anything slower. I've injected myself with the vaccine.

You can see what the result is.

Most of the food's in the car. Make use of it. It's about two months' worth, maybe more. Stay safe. Stay hidden. Stay away from the government. If there's any left, they're the ones to fear, not the dead."

Day 81, Grange Farm Estate, Hampshire

It's still raining. I want to leave. I want to go out and see for myself. All I have to do is follow the motorway south. And I've a car now. Two cars. I can easily make it. I've food, too. Months of food, enough to keep me going until the fruit can be picked from the trees. I need to know.

But in this rain, it would be impossible to see the road. Once again I'm stuck. Tomorrow, then. Tomorrow I'll go and I'll see.

Day 93, Brazely Abbey, Hampshire

This is beginning to look like a place people could live in. I've food, water, and a barricade around the buildings, and a second longer wall around the vegetable patch and orchard. It's not a great wall, but it's holding Them off. They come in ones and twos, a slow never-ending trickle, attracted by the sound of my labour. I let Them build up, then thin out their ranks every few hours. It doesn't take long. Yesterday there were only eighteen in the entire day, and only nine more arrived overnight.

On the eighty-third day it stopped raining. I headed south towards the coast and looked for one of the muster points for the evacuation.

I think that the undead avoid the place, for there is nothing there for Them. I saw their bodies, though. Individually to start with, then in clumps of two or three, then scores as I reached the fence. Their bodies were piled against it, as if They'd died climbing and clawing at the wire, trying to get inside.

These bodies were not as desiccated as those I've killed recently. They must have been killed during the evacuation process itself. Such a bloodless, misleading phrase *evacuation process*. The zombies must have gathered at the fence, more and more being drawn in by the sound of gunfire.

I didn't bother going in. Even from half a mile away, it was clear what had happened. Outside lay the few hundred zombies who'd followed the evacuees. Inside lay the evacuees themselves. Thousands upon thousands, their bodies mixed with those of the carrion birds that had come to feast upon them.

This is what Jen was protecting me from. What she knew would happen. What she thought had to happen. Yet I was, I am, one of the architects of this greatest of betrayals.

The logic is simple, elegant in its evil. There never was enough food to keep everyone alive, but those who were left to wander the streets, looking for the scraps left behind, would probably become infected, and thus the ranks of our enemy would grow. They had to be killed, murdered so that others might live. A great, and ultimately futile, sacrifice.

And that is not the worst of it. I was bitten as I returned. I was paying no heed to where I was going. My mind was fixed on what I'd seen, on the faces of the unnecessary dead, though I was yet to realise how truly unnecessary their murders had been. I was on foot when it attacked. It was small, but I could not say whether it was male or female, young or old. Its clothes were in tatters. Its legs were stumps that ended at its ankles. It had been hidden underneath a car, and before I'd realised it was there, it reached out and bit my leg.

My instincts have changed over these last months. Where once I would have screamed and panicked, now I brought the end of my pike down on its head with enough force to pierce the skull. Its skull cracked open, covering my feet and legs in a slick reddish ooze.

It was only a shallow wound, but it was infected, of that I had no doubt. Even if, by some lucky chance, I'd not been infected by its bite, as I stood there, numb from all I'd seen, I watched as its brain matter oozed down my leg, covering the small pricks of blood its bite had drawn.

I washed my legs and continued walking. There was no pain. There was no fear. I found a hill and sat, waiting for the sunset.

At dawn, I got up and came back here. That was six days ago.

I don't believe in luck, not anymore. Seven times since then, during the attacks on the abbey, when the numbers have been so great that the undead have breached the walls, I've been bitten. Seven times I've been bitten, and I have not turned. I examine my eyes in the mirror every morning and they remain unchanged, clear of those flecks of grey that have marked all the living dead that I have met. I am not infected, and I can't be the only one who is immune. How many countless others have died or been killed out of an erroneous fear that they were about to turn?

Fear. That was our undoing. I did not know the vaccine wasn't real, nor did I know that not everyone would become infected, but others must have. If I'd suggested that people should have barricaded their doors, that we should have ridden out the storm in our homes, I don't know if I'd have been listened to. All I know is that if we'd done that, millions who are now dead would have had a chance to survive.

As for what has become of those who decided on this final genocidal plan, I can only hope that the silence around me and in the skies above is their final testament.

Epilogue - 16th June

Day 96, Brazely Abbey, Hampshire

Not long after my last entry, which I had intended to be the final one, I realised that the answers to the question of why and how this all occurred lay within my grasp. They were in the files that my enigmatic friend, Sholto, had sent to me. I've carried my laptop and the hard drive all the way from London, but have never looked at what he sent. In truth, I've given it little thought. He'd asked me to keep them safe. That I had done, but to what end? Without power they were nothing more than a reminder of the friend that I had never met, yet whose loss I feel the most.

The laptop had less than thirty minutes of battery life left when I turned it on. It was enough to view one file, a video from a handheld camera.

The recording showed a room that I recognised. The ballroom from the Mount Clare Hotel in New York. Hotel is a misnomer, for the building is actually a private hospital. Technically, it belongs to the UN, and is used for the treatment of those foreign representatives which political animosity or international arrest warrants would prevent from being treated on U.S. soil.

The ballroom, not used for that purpose since the 1950s, was lit by harsh white lamps set up around the perimeter. The sofas and armchairs that I remembered from my tour of the building, when the room was used as a recovery area for the more mobile patients, were gone. In their place were two rows of hospital beds. On each was a patient, a drip running into one arm, an array of monitoring equipment to one side.

Walking between the beds were men and women, possibly nurses, checking drips, examining the monitors. To the rear of the room, away from the camera was a multi-ethnic cluster of suits. With them were a handful of nervous-looking military uniforms. Everyone wore masks, making identification difficult.

191

"Clear the room," one of the suits, a woman with a U.S. accent said.

"What about the guards?" another suit, male, British and familiar, asked.

"No need. The subjects are secure," the woman replied.

There was a pause as the soldiers left the room. The only sound, as the door closed behind the last one, was the quiet arrhythmic beeping of the life support monitors.

"Are we ready, Doctor?" the American asked.

The camera panned across the room. There were fourteen patients, fifteen nurses, one doctor, one camera operator and about two-dozen suits. Nine stood near the beds; behind each, craning their necks to get a good view, hovered one or two aides.

"Ladies and Gentlemen," the doctor said, a faint trace of India still detectable in his English accent, "I need to warn you that when the agent is administered, the patients will spasm and convulse. This is normal. We have seen this in all of our tests so far. Do not be alarmed. However, for your own safety, please stand back." The doctor looked around the group once more. "All of these patients had at least one of the viruses on the list. All were within a few weeks of death. We have infected them with the remaining viruses detailed on page four of your briefing papers."

One of the suits pointedly glanced at his watch impatiently.

The doctor distractedly raised a hand to wipe at his masked mouth. "Without the administering of this compound, there is not one of these patients who will be alive at the end of the week—"

"Yes, Doc, we know that, we're not some ethics board you need to justify yourself to. Get on with it," the American said.

"Yes, ma'am." The doctor nodded to the nurses. They positioned themselves so that one nurse stood by each bed. The doctor walked over to the last remaining nurse who opened a refrigerated crate and took out a box. Together they went around the beds handing out a syringe to each nurse, one for each patient.

"Mark the time," the doctor said, "05:00 EST." He looked over at the suits. The American woman looked over at the Brit.

"Go on," the Brit said. "It's what we've all come here for, isn't it?"

"Go," the American echoed.

"05:00 and five seconds. Go," the doctor said. The nurses injected the contents of the syringe into the patients' drips.

"Well?" the Brit asked after a minute.

"It takes time, sir," the doctor said.

"How long? We need this to be fast-acting, or else what's the point of a super-vaccine?"

"A few minutes to enter the blood stream, a few more to begin acting, perhaps five before we start to see a change. That will be in the patients' blood work, you understand," the doctor went on, his voice relaxed now that, to all intents and purposes, his job was done. "This will not repair the organ damage. These patients will not regain consciousness and they will still die, but when we examine their blood you will see that the compounds with which we infected them are no longer present."

"You mean we're not going to see them get up off the table and walk again?" the American asked.

"So what the hell are we doing here?" the Brit snapped, tearing off his mask. "For Christ's sake man, you said we'd see a miracle here!"

"We will. You will," the doctor said hurriedly, the tremor back in his voice. "This compound is eighty-percent effective against the viruses you listed. Within a matter of weeks we can adapt it to any unknown pathogen. With more work, more time, we can reduce that to a matter of days."

"In my experience," a suit with a Chinese accent said, "when a scientist asks for more time, they are really asking for more funding. Now, if you will excuse me, my plane is waiting and I am due back in Beijing."

One of the patients began to convulse. "Ah, as we expected," the doctor said, relief creeping into his voice. "The battle for the man's life, our agent against the viruses—"

"Spare us, Doctor," another suit, with a far stronger Indian accent than the doctor's, said caustically. "We all have matters of state to attend to. Send us the report. When there is something *to* report."

"Then, ladies, gentlemen," the Brit began, "we should all get out of here before—"

The slow, steady beat of the heart monitors was suddenly drowned out by a high-pitched single flat tone. The doctor hurried over to the bed. He reached it at the same time as the patient, contradicting the equipment, sat up.

"Nurse, I need—" But before the doctor could finish the sentence the patient reached out and grabbed at the man, pulled him close, and bit down on his hand. The doctor fell to the floor, clutching his wrist, blood pouring from the stubs of his two missing fingers.

There was a flurry of shouting and swearing, of calls for the guards, for someone to open the doors, and above them all, a cacophony of screams for help.

One of the suits, cursing in Spanish, pushed her way through the crowd backing away from the patient and the wounded doctor. She picked up the ECG monitor and heaved it down onto the patient's head. She took a step back and slapped her hands together with that universal gesture of a job, done. The patient in the next bed sat up, grabbed her, pulled her closer, and tore at her arm.

The camera operator, another attendant in blue hospital scrubs, ran across the shot, heading straight for the locked door. The camera must have been on a tripod, because through its steady lens, I watched as one after another, the rest of the patients sat up. They grabbed at the nurses now trapped in the space between the beds. They grabbed at the suits trying to get to the doors. They bit. They tore. They infected. And the doors remained closed.

Finally, seven minutes after the patients had been injected, the doors opened. There can't have been any security cameras in that ballroom, because they were opened by a solitary soldier who appeared confused, not scared. As soon as the doors opened, the occupants of the room fled, leaving the undead patients and a dozen dead or dying suits and scrubs behind.

That was when the battery finally ran out.

The British suit, the one who took off his mask, him I recognised. It was Sir Michael Quigley, our foreign secretary. The man who took over the country after the PM was ousted.

The super-vaccine that was promised to our evacuees never existed because it was the vaccine itself which started this plague. Our leadership knew this. I had wondered why we were never invaded, why no foreign Special Forces units were sent in to raid the factories where our vaccine was being made. Of course, they knew the truth. So did the foreign secretary, our leader in those last days before the collapse.

Having seen that footage, I now feel that all my life had been a lie. All that time I was just another pawn in someone else's game, not the kingmaker I'd always seen myself as.

I haven't been able to view the other files, not yet. Without power, I've no way of recharging the computer, but there is one in particular I want to look at. It's titled 'Lenham Hill Trials'. I knew I'd seen the name somewhere. I must have read the name when I downloaded the files. I don't know what I expect to see, or what I will get out of viewing them. Closure? Hardly.

Perhaps all I want is to understand how this could have happened. Perhaps if I can understand the mistakes of the past, then, in some small way, I can prevent them from being repeated. Perhaps not, but after discovering my, albeit unwitting, involvement in the genocide that was the evacuation, I feel a responsibility to the other survivors.

I am sure they are out there, and sure that I will meet them. If we know the truth of the past then we not-so-meek who have inherited this diseased Earth can build something better upon it. Perhaps.

The end.

Printed in Great Britain
by Amazon